MW00966687

"One of my favourite titles in the series is **Aquarius**. […] I loved this book." — Camilla During, *freelance reviewer*

Be Counted: "the narrative, written in diary form, is exciting and readable. […] a vivid sketch of a moment in history when women's and girls' horizons were being broadened."— Trevor Agnew, *Magpies*

Beneath the Mountains: "a great story set in the 1930s […] an awesome book, all written through the eyes of a 14-year-old…" — Child reviewer, *The Northern Advocate*

A Better Life: "a marvellous introduction to life in Northland in the 1920s" — Trevor Agnew, *Magpies*

Castaway: "an exciting, convincing, fascinating tale of hardship and survival. […] The story is gripping in its unrelenting depiction of the day to day survival of a varied cast of characters in extraordinary, inhospitable surroundings." — *NZ Post judges' report*

Chinatown Girl: "The latest book in this outstanding series by Scholastic […] brings to life an important but little-known aspect of our history." — 'e.g.', *NZ Herald*

Cyclone Bola: "… a fascinating read; […] keeps you turning pages as Amy's exciting tale unfolds. [Includes] photographs of damage to give readers an idea of just how destructive the cyclone really was." — *Tierney, Christchurch Kids Blog*

Earthquake: "Napier in the 1930s was a time of going without. Then, in February 1931, disaster strikes the small town … an earthquake that destroys the school and much of the town centre." — *Kiwireviews*

Escape from Sarau: "For me this was a non-stop read. I knew nothing of German/Lutheran settlers and found Emilie's fictional diary quite fascinating." — *Talespinners*

Fire in the Sky: "The dramatic happenings around Lake Tarawera during the eruption of 1886 are vividly brought to life in this story. […] The attitudes and prejudices of the times show clearly …"
— *Around the Bookshops*

Gold: "plenty of suspense […] Cartwright strikes the right balance of historical detail and adventure plot …" — *Otago Daily Times*

Gumdigger: "a fascinating glimpse into the hardships of daily life in northern New Zealand at the end of the 19th century. […] photographs, map and historical notes put Reuben's diary into historical perspective. A valuable addition to the series."
— Julie Harper, *Magpies*

Here Come the Marines: "a terrific insight into a life that, although only two generations ago, must seem like a thousand years ago for any young person reading it. It is a valuable insight for any teenager studying this period in history. Recommended for ages 10–110."
— *Local Matters, Mahurangi*

Journey to Tangiwai: "This is an awesome book. I thoroughly enjoyed reading it. It gets better every time you read it (I have read it three times). I highly recommend it – 9½ out of 10."
— Child reviewer, *Wairarapa Times-Age*

Kauri in My Blood: "Orwin's in-depth knowledge of the kauri timber industry provides considerable detail to this fictional diary. The rough nature of the living conditions and the camaraderie of the crews working in the camps is well portrayed. A valuable addition to a well-respected and popular series." — Julie Harper, *Magpies*

Land of Promise: "This must be one of the best early settler stories I have read – I have read it twice." — *Around the Bookshops*

The Mine's Afire: "'Compelling' is the word for 'The Mine's Afire!' – another in the My Story series that takes young readers to the heart of turning points in our history." — *Dominion Post*

Mission Girl: "The author skilfully uses Atapo's story, which is exciting in itself, to fill in many historical as well as domestic details of every day life in Paihia in the months leading up to the signing of the Treaty."
— *Around the Bookshops*

No Survivors: "… a great snapshot of New Zealand that will bring to life the highs and lows of 1979. […] Sharon Holt has created an entertaining read that recounts with respect the events of the Mt Erebus disaster." — *Christine Hurst*

Pandemic: "Spanish Flu ravaged the world after WWI and killed 8600 people in New Zealand […] the story […] will astound today's kids who are not used to being seen but not heard. […] excellent photographs and a historical timeline. This is just brilliant." — *Bob Docherty*

"**Sabotage!** very effectively combines history and mystery within an accessible diary format. It is well paced and readers will relate well to the characters." — *Magpies*

Sitting on the Fence: "Nagelkerke's accurate, well researched novel is a convincing evocation of the [1981 Springbok] tour, its time and place, and especially the divisive impact it had on society. It's a book that places the reader firmly in history's frontline – complete with batons and barbed wire."
— *NZ Post Judges' Report 2008*

The Wahine Disaster: "This is a highly readable account of a 12 year old girl's reactions not only to the horrors of the disaster but also to the day by day events of the late 1960s." — *Around the Bookshops*

"I am writing to say how much I have enjoyed reading your My Story series. Quite often, after making my way through an adult non-fiction book I turn my eyes for lighter stuff to the young people's section in the library. […] Chinatown Girl was the first I read and became fascinated by her life. […] So keen was I to read more My Stories I hunted the library shelves for them and have since read 8 different ones. […] Each story is different, compelling too, and conveys a young person's thoughts and feelings of their time, centred round historical events. Makes history come to life." — *Elizabeth, adult reader*

Titles in the *My Story/My New Zealand Story* series

My New Zealand Story

CANTERBURY QUAKE

Christchurch, 2010-11   Desna Wallace

Desna W_____ 2014

SCHOLASTIC
AUCKLAND SYDNEY NEW YORK LONDON TORONTO
MEXICO CITY NEW DELHI HONG KONG

First published in 2014 by Scholastic New Zealand Limited
Private Bag 94407, Greenmount, Auckland 1730, New Zealand

Scholastic Australia Pty Limited
PO Box 579, Gosford, NSW 2250, Australia

© Desna Wallace, 2014

ISBN 968-1-77543-182-4

National Library of New Zealand Cataloguing-in-Publication Data

Wallace, Desna.
Canterbury Quake : Christchurch, 2010-11 / by Desna Wallace.
(My New Zealand story)
ISBN 978-1-77543-182-4 (pbk.)—ISBN 978-1-77543-229-6 (ebk.)
1.Canterbury Earthquake, N.Z., 2010—Juvenile fiction. 2. Christchurch
Earthquake, N.Z., 2011—Juvenile fiction. 3. Christchurch (N.Z.)—
Juvenile fiction. [1. Canterbury Earthquake, N.Z., 2010—Fiction.
2. Christchurch Earthquake, N.Z., 2011—Fiction. 3. Girls—Fiction
4. Diary fiction. 5. Earthquakes—Fiction. 6. Christchurch (N.Z.)—Fiction].
I. Title. II. Series.
NZ823.3—dc 23

9 8 7 6 5 4 3 2 1   4 5 6 7 8 9/ 1

This title is also available as an ebook.

Publishing team: Diana Murray, Lynette Evans, Penny Scown and Frith Hughes
Front cover photograph by Marty Melville, Getty Images; back cover photograph from
    Wikimedia Commons, Marin Luff
Design: Book Design Ltd, www.bookdesign.co.nz
Typeset in Helvetica Neue Regular 10/16.5
Printed in Singapore by Tien Wah Press (PTE) Ltd

Every effort has been made to trace all copyright holders of material in this book. If any rights have been omitted, the publishers offer their sincere apologies and will rectify this in any subsequent edition following notification.

To my son,
CALVIN WAKELY
Love always

Acknowledgments

This book would not be in your hands today if it wasn't for the support of so many people. Thank you to Kathy Ross who gave me the push I needed. To the wonderful team at Scholastic New Zealand, especially Diana Murray, Penny Scown and Frith Hughes; my heartfelt thanks for your patience and expertise.

To my son Calvin Wakely and his fiancée Bryar Luscombe who told me not only that I should write this book, but that I could write this book. Thank you for believing in me.

There is one more important group that I must thank and that is the children of Fendalton Open-Air School who inspire me every day. After the February earthquake I began a book club for Year Six students to have something positive to focus on instead of the continual disruptions to our lives. We called ourselves the Faultline Fiction Fanatics and I thank all of you for sharing your stories, your fears, up days and down days, after the February earthquake. Thank you! You made the toughest year more bearable. Without you all, this book would not have been possible.

— *Desna Wallace*

SUNDAY, 8 AUGUST 2010

I've been dropping hints for ages. Heaps and heaps! I've left pictures of cell phones all over the place. I've stuck them on the fridge and even on the back of the toilet door. Tessa tells me I'm wasting my time. She says I'm not going to get a cell phone until I'm thirteen. She had to wait until then so I should too. Then she deliberately texted her friends in front of me, just to make her point.

Well, I don't care what Tessa says. Thirteen is too far away and I am not going to give up. If everyone else at school has a cell phone, then I want one too! Even my best friend Laura has one, so I desperately need one. How am I supposed to know what everyone is up to if I don't have my own phone?

TUESDAY, 10 AUGUST

Only three more days until my eleventh birthday. I can hardly wait. Surely turning 11 is a good enough reason to get a cell phone? I rang Aunty Beth tonight and begged her to help. Mum always listens to her sister, even if she is younger than Mum.

"Yes! Maddy, I'll try. I promise," she said. "But you know your mum. If she says no, she means no."

I know Aunty Beth is probably right, but I really want a phone soooo bad. Why can't Mum see that? Everyone at school has one. I'm going to Intermediate next year and I just **have** to have one. I'll have to think of another way to convince her.

FRIDAY, 13 AUGUST
My birthday!

I woke up early and was all excited and hopeful. I mean, who wouldn't wake up early on their birthday? But my hopefulness didn't last long. No cell phone. I can't believe it. It's so not fair. In fact, it sucks.

The day wasn't a total waste though. Actually everyone was pretty nice. Even Tessa made me a card and gave me some new pens and paper. And we did have pizza for dinner. Home-delivered pizza, not the awful stuff from the supermarket that comes frozen in a box. Mum and Dad gave me a set of beads to make friendship bracelets, a box of chocolates, and a book voucher from my favourite bookshop and promised me we would go shopping tomorrow. I hope the shop has the new vampire book I've been waiting for.

SATURDAY, 14 AUGUST

Saturday – and money to spend. Woohoo! We all piled into Dad's car and parked around the back of the shops. I love going to the bookshop in Victoria Street. There are so many books to choose from. Jackson spent all his time playing with the trains in the corner, while I spent ages looking at books, even though I found the one I wanted straight away.

Then we were allowed to choose a cupcake from the cupcake parlour across the road. Dad's was chocolate with chocolate icing and chocolate sprinkles. Talk about chocolate overkill. And of course Jackson wanted one like Dad's, too. Mum chose a raspberry one. Tessa and I both went for cupcakes with heaps and heaps of pink icing and strawberries on top. After buying the cupcakes we went to the cheese shop and bought fresh baked bread and yummy cheese. I don't know how Mum and Dad can eat the blue cheese they bought. Ugh! Looks mouldy and I bet it tastes mouldy too. That's one thing Tessa and I agree on. Probably the only thing. Mouldy cheese is not for us.

We then walked a bit further in to Victoria Square and sat by the Avon River and just enjoyed a bit of time out. It was a good day, even if I didn't get a cell phone. I won't give up though. I still want one. My mission will not be over until I get a cell phone!

SUNDAY, 15 AUGUST

Laura came over so we spent the day just hanging out. We tried making our own cupcakes but got more icing over the floor than on the cakes. Jackson was just being a pain, following us everywhere. And he never stops talking. Laura got a text from her Mum to say she was allowed to stay longer because her Mum and Dad were still out shopping and would pick her up at about half-past four.

"See, Mum!" I said, "There's a good reason to have a cell phone. Laura's Mum can contact her if plans change."

Mum just ignored me. Tessa, who happened to be in the room, grinned and texted her friend. She did it deliberately, like she always does. I hate her sometimes.

Laura stuck a candle in one of the cupcakes and sang happy birthday to me and then and gave me a birthday present. It was a CD she'd made of our favourite songs. Cool! We played it over and over until her parents came and picked her up.

MONDAY, 16 AUGUST

We had choir practice today. I think it went well. I just love singing so much. We are learning a heap of new songs. Laura and I are trying out for the duet for the final assembly at Christmas. She's much better than I am and is heaps more confident, but when we sing together it makes me feel as though I'm singing okay, too. And I have more fun singing with her. The intermediate school we are going to next year has a big focus on music and drama. That's mostly why we're going there. The drama and music teachers from the intermediate come and check out the performances at our end of year assembly. They do it every year to get an idea of what we are all like. I guess they do it so they know what they are going to get the following year. I will be terrified and excited at the same time. I so want us to get the final duet. I sooo want to get in the music and drama classes next year.

THURSDAY, 19 AUGUST

It was my day to do library duty at lunchtime, and we got to stamp the new books. It's a good chance to see the new books before anyone else. We even get to reserve them before all the other kids get a chance to see them. It's one of the reasons I like doing library. Plus it's warm inside in winter. Like today, the library was really busy at lunch because it was so cold outside. But it gets so noisy. Sometimes I am sure my brain hurts because of all the noise, as half the school is squashed into the library trying to stay warm. It's okay for the teachers because they can go into the staffroom for lunch, while we have to walk around outside in winter. So not fair!

When I got home, there was a flyer in the letterbox advertising cell phones on special. I left it by Mum's bed. She used it to light the fire. Typical! I know she did it on purpose. I can't win with her. She just won't budge. Being 11 is a whole 2 years away from 13. I'll be so old by then, that by the time I get one, they'll be obsolete. We'll be talking to each other with just our thoughts and won't need any technological stuff. Actually, that could be kind of freaky. We'd never be able to have any secrets. On second thoughts, I don't think I would like that at all.

FRIDAY, 20 AUGUST

Yay! No homework for the weekend. Plenty of time to hang out with Laura and sing, eat and watch DVDs. Our all time favourite is the DVD of *Glee* with all the high school students singing in class. It's a little bit geeky and the actors are way older than what they are pretending to be, but the singing is fantastic. I could watch it over and over again.

SATURDAY, 21 AUGUST

Laura came over for lunch so we could practise our song. I kept forgetting the words halfway through. I don't think Laura was impressed after about our 10th attempt. She just gave me one of her 'not again' looks. I told her she looked like my mother when she did that and we both burst out laughing. Lucky I remembered on the next go and we sang it all the way through without any stopping or wrong words. We really need to do well with the duet if we want to get in to the music and drama class next year and be part of the school productions. First, though, we have to pass the auditions to get to do the final assembly duet. Both of us have had times when we have led the choir into a major song so there is always hope. Mind you, Zoe and Bettina – two other girls from year six – could be trouble for us. Especially Zoe. Sometimes she is so mean to me. It's like she is bullying me, but on the sly so that the teachers don't notice. I know it was her foot that tripped me up in PE the other day. And I KNOW it was deliberate.

SUNDAY, 22 AUGUST

Today I went to Laura's place for lunch. I love going to Laura's house. Her house is on Avonside Drive overlooking the Avon River and it is so pretty. It's full of nooks and crannies and all these antique things. Her parents collect things from everywhere they go and they went to heaps of countries before Laura was born so they have all these weird souvenirs. Everything is so random but so awesome. Her Dad is cool and very funny

– he makes all sorts of faces every time Laura turns her back on him.

We made chocolate mud cake . . . and another mess. We are pretty good at making messes. I think we would be top of the class for making a mess. Today it was mostly the icing that was messy. Her Dad said the mess was the biggest he had ever seen. He said the kitchen looked like something from the bottom of the sea, "all sludgy and brown." Then he pulled the silliest face when he thought Laura wasn't looking but she saw him and started chasing him around the kitchen trying to flick him with the tea towel. He grabbed a tea towel too and they had a flick fight. Laura's parents are so much fun. I'm sure it's because she has no brothers or sisters. Sometimes I wish I was an only kid, especially when Tessa is being bossy and Jackson is following me around. But only sometimes!

WEDNESDAY, 25 AUGUST

We were given so much homework today. Our teacher, Miss Higgins, always goes overboard. She gives us maths, spelling and current events as well as heaps more. Laura calls her 'Miss Overboard', but not to her face of course. The teacher must think we don't have any sort of life other than just doing her homework. We get a week to do it but I like to get it done early so I don't have any to do on the weekend. I rang Laura when I got stuck on the book review because I'd left the book at school and couldn't remember the author's name or any other books she had written, and we weren't allowed to use the computer for this part of the homework. Mum wanted the phone so I couldn't talk long and now I probably won't get a good mark on the homework sheet. I pointed out to Mum that if I had a cell phone I could text Laura for help. All I got was another blank stare. She is sooo stubborn. Mind you, she says I'm stubborn – and persistent too. Hmmm. Maybe there's hope then, if I keep trying.

SATURDAY, 28 AUGUST

I wanted to spend today with Laura but we had to visit Gran. Dad mowed her lawns and Mum made us all do chores. Gran is okay – in fact she is pretty cool for an old person – but I really wished I could've been at Laura's. We know all our words off by heart now for our duet but I still want to practise. I wish I didn't get so nervous. I don't know how Laura can stand up there so calmly.

"Take long, slow breaths," she says.

If I took a long, slow breath I would end up with hiccups – or I'd pass out. Then I would never be able to sing.

SUNDAY, 29 AUGUST

Today was movie day. Laura and I went to the Hoyts movie place next to Science Alive in town. Tessa and her friend Rosie came too. I don't think Mum trusts us by ourselves. Sometimes she is so overprotective it drives me nuts. At least we didn't have to take Jackson. Dragging a 5-year-old around would be too much and it wouldn't be fair. The movie was okay but not the best we had seen. It was more fun playing at Time Out after. I beat Tessa at air hockey three times. Yes! Yes! And yes! Any chance to beat Tessa and I am in.

MONDAY, 30 AUGUST

Miss Finch, the choir teacher, pulled Laura and me aside after practice today. I thought we were in trouble but she just wanted to let us know she thought we were doing fine. She asked us if we wanted do a song for assembly on the 24th of September. That's the last day of term. It will be like a sort of try-out for the end of year assembly. We just looked at each other and said, "Do we?" at the same time and then got the giggles.

"I'll take that as a yes," she said, laughing. Then she said Zoe and Bettina were also going to do a song and suddenly I didn't feel so excited any more. They are really good singers. They're our competition so we will have to practise even more.

TUESDAY, 31 AUGUST

We spent all lunchtime going through CDs and listening to songs we might want to sing. Laura wanted something jazzy and I wanted something a bit more pop. We just ended up arguing, so in the end Miss Finch made the decision for us. We're going to sing 'Daydream Believer', which is an old song from the 1960s, but we can do it like they did on *Glee*. It was just brilliant.

WEDNESDAY, 1 SEPTEMBER

Practise, practise, practise! Sing, sing, sing! Roll on Saturday, and a chance to get it right.

SATURDAY, 4 SEPTEMBER
EARTHQUAKE!!!! 4.35 a.m.

I think I am in shock and I'm almost too scared to write in my diary because then it would mean what happened today was true and I don't want it to be true. I don't want it to have happened at all, but I need to write it down because it is just so horrendous.

In the middle of the night, when we were all sleeping, the most terrifying thing happened. From somewhere deep below us the ground began rumbling. It was a rumble and a roar so loud that it woke us all and woke the whole city and maybe the whole of New Zealand. It was a rumble that went on and on, and grew louder and louder. Then everything was moving, shaking, falling, banging and crashing.

I could hear Jackson screaming. Mum and Dad were yelling at us to get under the doorway. I tried getting out of bed but got thrown to the floor. I thought I was going to throw up, my stomach was churning so much from all the movement. I couldn't stand up straight. The noise, the sound of things smashing and banging and breaking was deafening. I was so frightened. It was just so awful and it came out of nowhere.

Then suddenly Tessa was next to me and helped me up. Dad grabbed us both and shoved us under the doorframe. We clung on madly. Things were still falling, tumbling, crashing. Something was banging all over the roof, really loud and heavy. It echoed through the whole house. I thought the roof was going to cave in. The house was shaking like we were caught up in a food blender, going around and around.

Mum and Jackson were under the doorframe of his room and he just kept screaming. I was so scared. The noise was horrendous. It was so loud and so scary and it just went on and on. It sounded like a train was going to come through the front walls. Then, everything stopped.

There was just silence and the thump-thumping of my own heart beating. Then everything went dark. Really dark!

No power. Now we were in complete darkness. We scrambled to the lounge banging into things that had fallen. I stubbed my toes so many times. I was crying and so scared. I have never been so scared. I don't know how to describe it. It was just horrible, and the noise is still in my head. Jackson stopped screaming but then he started whimpering and Mum kept telling him he was okay.

"It's just an earthquake," she told him. "We'll be okay."

I didn't believe her, not really. Tessa looked scared too. We all did. I have never felt anything like that in my life and I NEVER want to go through that again. Ever!

I don't know how Dad managed it in the dark but somehow he found the torch. When he shone it around the lounge all we could see was mess and broken things strewn everywhere.

Dad went in to the kitchen and tried the taps and the lights. No water. No power. "Stay here," he said, "I'm going to check on Mrs Williams next door. Poor old dear will be terrified."

The rest of us just stood there waiting until he got back. It didn't take long before he brought her into the lounge. Even in the dark, I could tell she'd been crying and that she was as scared as we were.

Mum fumbled to find blankets and sleeping bags from the hall cupboard and threw them at us. "Keep yourselves warm while Dad and I look around the house."

Then there was another huge rumbling and roaring and the shaking began all over again. I screamed. I didn't mean to, but I couldn't help it. It just came out. Then I burst into tears, and so did Tessa.

Mum and Dad came running and stumbling back and we all stayed in the lounge with Jackson whimpering all the rest of the night. The whole time we stayed there the ground just kept rolling. Sometimes it would shake, noisy and loud. Other times the ground rolled up and down like we were on a little boat being tossed around at sea. It was the most awful, awful night ever. Dad tried to make us laugh and told us stories but it didn't really work. Mum kept trying to ring Aunty Beth and Gran. It was ages before she got through because the phones were overloaded with everyone trying to check on each other.

In the daylight it wasn't any better. The ground just kept on shaking and rolling. Dad took heaps of photos of all the things that had smashed on the floor. Then we picked up all the broken glass and crockery. Even the tomato sauce had fallen out of the pantry and oozed out onto the carpet. It looked like blood and made me feel sick.

Mrs Williams' son came and took her back to his house. I don't think she will be back for a while. Her house is all messed up like ours, but she lives on her own and is older than Gran so shouldn't be on her own while this is happening.

Out in the street, all the neighbours stood around talking most of the day. There's still no power, so no TV to see how bad things are in the rest of the city. Dad has been listening on the car radio though, and the news is not good. It was a massive 7.1 magnitude earthquake near Darfield, just outside Christchurch. Lots of houses have been damaged and some have collapsed almost completely. I can't believe it. I just cannot believe it. It makes me feel sick. Dad did say that most of Christchurch does have power, which is good, but not where we are yet.

Because we haven't got any water, Dad's dug a hole in the garden and says we have to go to the toilet out there. Ugh! Gross! Disgusting! Dad put up some tarpaulin so we could have some privacy. Privacy! Huh. There's no privacy when you're peeing in a hole in the ground outside. Tessa stands guard for me and I stand guard for her.

There's this muddy stuff all over the garden and street. Dad didn't know what it was but one of our neighbours, Mr Tyson says it's liquefaction, whatever that is. It's an awful, horrible grey stuff. He said it's pretty bad in places and had caused flooding on many streets. He said he'd been over to his family in Ilam and they had power and water. He also said he'd seen the news and the Mayor said there was a state of emergency. That means heaps of people from Civil Defence, the army and everywhere else are coming to help. All these emergency workers makes it all so real.

Oh no! Dusty, I haven't seen my cat, Dusty. She's always nearby. She never leaves the property and I know she'll be scared too. Mum says she'll turn up when she feels a bit safer. Cats are good at hiding, she said. I hope she's okay. I miss her.

Dad and I drove over to Gran's and brought her back to stay with us for a while. The trip took ages because the roads are messed up – either flooded, caked with liquefaction, or blocked off completely. We ran into heaps of roadblocks. Gran's house is okay but none of us want her to be on her own. We all need to be together right now.

SUNDAY, 5 SEPTEMBER

We didn't get much sleep last night – just sat talking and jumping with fright every time the ground shook, which was pretty much all night. Dad said they were aftershocks and would stop soon. He reckons the biggest one is over so we'll be okay now. I'm not sure if he believes it himself. I was sooo tired that I didn't mind curling up in my sleeping bag next to Tessa and Jackson on the lounge floor. I wouldn't tell Tessa, but I'm too scared to sleep in my own bed anyway. Actually Gran slept in my bed. Even Mum and Dad and Aunty Beth and Uncle

Dave slept on the floor, not that any of us slept much – so many aftershocks.

Today we started clearing up bricks. The noises on the roof last night was the chimney collapsing and tumbling down. The bricks were all over the drive, in the garden, and on top of Mum's car, which was dented all over. When Mum looked at all the bricks, I thought she was going to cry. "My daffodils are all ruined," she told Dad. "They'd only just flowered and now they've all been crushed." Dad hugged her and then we all hugged each other. It felt good.

We still have no power or water and we still have to go to the toilet in the garden. Jackson thinks it is fun peeing in the garden. I don't. It's disgusting.

Some of the neighbours have already started packing things in their cars. I think they might be leaving Christchurch or going to stay on the other side of town where they have power and water. Mr Henry on the other side of us said there had apparently been heaps and heaps of damage, especially in the city centre, and lots of buildings had fallen down. Mum just kept saying it was amazing that no one died. The day seemed so long, without power or water, and with mess everywhere. And all day the ground kept shaking.

Aunty Beth and Uncle Dave came over and Dad and Uncle Dave climbed up on the roof and pulled down the rest of chimney. Brick by brick, it took ages, and then they put a tarpaulin over the hole in the roof. "We don't need rain ruining the carpet on top of everything else," Mum said.

Aunty Beth's house is surrounded by liquefaction, so they're going to stay with us now too. They had to dig out the driveway just to get the car out.

It is lucky we have one of the old-style phones as modern-day ones need power. I haven't spoken to Laura yet. Mum says to use the phone only for emergencies. I reckon it is an emergency because I don't know how Laura is.

With the aftershocks, it's the noise that comes first. It just sneaks up on you, loud and angry. It is so crazy to see the walls rocking back and forth. So scary – and so unbelievably loud. It's like a jet engine roar that comes out of nowhere and just gets louder and louder and then stops suddenly. I wish it would stop forever.

I think Mother Nature is having a massive tantrum and stamping her feet, and we are the ones getting stomped on.

Dusty is still missing.

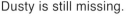

MONDAY, 6 SEPTEMBER

No school today. No anything. Some shops are shut but mostly things like supermarkets are open. By the time I got up, Dad had been down to our local dairy to buy water and milk. We already have cereal and bread. He bought a newspaper, too, and the photos were awful.

I couldn't believe what some parts of town look like.

We got power this afternoon. Yahoo! The water also came back on but we have to boil it before using it just in case it's contaminated with sewerage and stuff. Ewww! Even when we brush our teeth, we have to use boiled water. We sat in front of the TV most of the day, watching the news. There are soldiers all over town trying to keep people out of the central city. Many of the older buildings in there have been damaged. There's debris all over the streets, and all over the cars in the streets. Earthquake reports were on TV most of the day. Mum wouldn't let Jackson watch and she didn't want me to watch either, but Dad said I could. I couldn't believe what I was watching and I couldn't believe no one had died. With all those bricks and damaged buildings and mess everywhere, it will take forever to clean up.

I finally got through to Laura on the phone today and we talked for ages. Her house is bad. It has huge cracks in the walls and lots of liquefaction. She said everyone in her street just got stuck in and started digging the stuff out from their driveways and the road where she lives.

Aunty Beth and Uncle Dave are still here. Their house is in Pacific Park, Bexley, one of the worst affected areas. They still don't have power or water. The liquefaction is so bad there they have to get diggers for some houses. Uncle Dave is so angry. He keeps saying, "It's a new bloody house. It shouldn't be damaged. The bloody council is to blame." Mum tells him to stop swearing but I know she agrees with him.

Dad went out today and brought back a few of Gran's things. Her house is not bad but she doesn't like being alone, so she's going to stay a bit longer. I wouldn't want to be on my own either. I'm so glad we're still all sleeping on the lounge floor. It's crowded and Jackson whimpers in his sleep then wakes up screaming from nightmares, but at least we are together. I sleep in my clothes ready to run if I have to. Dad swears a lot, like Uncle Dave. Normally Mum would have a go at him for swearing, but not these days.

Dusty is still missing. Mum just doesn't get it and says she's just a cat. But she is NOT just a cat. She's family and she is scared and I will keep looking for her until I find her. I keep calling for her up and down the street but she doesn't come. I'm really worried.

TUESDAY, 7 SEPTEMBER

Still no school. And Mum got a phone call today from her boss to tell her that their hairdressing shop in town has collapsed. Everything inside is ruined and she now has no job. Her boss can't pay her if he doesn't have a shop. I caught her crying when she thought I wasn't looking. I feel really helpless but there's nothing I can do.

Mum and Gran spend a lot of time talking, and having cups of tea. Dad had to go to work. He works on the roads and there's heaps to do. Jackson just watches DVDs but if he's left alone he starts being stupid and yelling. Tessa and I talk a bit more now, but mostly she just texts her friends. I wish I could see Laura, but with everything happening and the roads all messed up with liquefaction, we have to stay home.

Watching the news, it looks like Kaiapoi and places out that way were hit really hard too. One of my teachers lives out there. I hope she's okay.

Now that most of the shops are open, people are stocking up because the main warehouse where they keep the food supplies – which is on the other side of the city, in Hornby – got so damaged that everything is ruined. Everyone is panic-buying but the mayor says there's no need to, as there will be plenty for everyone as new stuff is being trucked in to the city.

Since the earthquake I have written so much in this diary I can hardly believe it, but there's always something happening, and with so many people in the house now, it is getting really crowded. It's hard to find a quiet place to write, but it does make me feel better when I do get to write things down. A couple of times I've hidden in the old glasshouse even though it's a bit smashed up and cold inside. At least it is quiet and gives me a chance to be alone.

WEDNESDAY, 8 SEPTEMBER

Wow! There was another big aftershock this morning. It was a big 5.2 shock, just before 8 this morning. Mum was on the phone when suddenly the rumble came again, out of nowhere, and she threw the phone on the floor and we all scrambled under the kitchen table. We don't need to be told any more. We drop down and get under the table or a doorway, or just drop to the floor like turtles with our head tucked under until the shaking stops. It's the noise I hate the most. The growling is so loud and so angry.

In the paper today, they said that schools would be closed until the 13th. I can't believe I'm saying this, but I really wish I was at school. I wish everything was the way it was before. I even miss arguing with Tessa. She's been so nice since the earthquakes, it's just a bit weird. People keep saying there is a chance we could have a big aftershock. I can't bear thinking about it.

Dad is at work all day and doing heaps of extra hours working on the roads. There are huge holes everywhere. Grey liquefaction is piled up like mountains up and down the roads. All over our side of town, but especially where Aunty Beth lives, there are students from the university digging up the liquefaction. It's so cool what they are doing. They found out about helping through a Facebook page someone set up, and everyone kept sharing messages until there were hundreds of them turning up in gumboots, ready to start shovelling.

There are pictures in the paper of the students. There are also pictures of the damaged houses and roads. Dad says it will take years to fix the roads. We're very lucky here, with only a little bit of liquefaction compared to other places in the city, but the dust is just everywhere. It's in the house and in the carpet and I can feel it in my hair. Gross.

Every day we have aftershocks. And every day the aftershocks do more damage. Lots of houses have had big red stickers put on their doors. It means their house is not safe to live in. I'm so glad our house is okay. Even though it's a bit damaged, at least we don't have to move out. Dad says it is all safe and our foundations are good.

THURSDAY, 9 SEPTEMBER

More shakes, more growling, roaring and rumbling from deep below in the earth. I HATE it.

Dusty is still missing. No matter how many times I go up and down the street calling, and looking in bushes and under hedges, I still can't find her. I hope she is okay. I miss her so much. I made a poster on the computer with a photo of her and our phone number and address on it and dropped copies in people's letterboxes. But no one has rung us. We got a few notices in our letterbox from other people who have lost pets too. It is so sad that so many animals are missing.

Dad bought us our own torch to keep by our beds. Straight after the big earthquake everyone was trying to buy batteries but they sold out everywhere. It seems so weird to have to keep torches by our beds ready for emergencies. It's not something I really thought about before.

FRIDAY, 10 SEPTEMBER

I tried writing a poem last night, when I couldn't sleep. I called it 'Tantrum'.

SHAKEN FROM SLEEP
THROWN FROM BED
A TORTURED SCREAM
MY OWN.
FEAR RUNS THROUGH MY VEINS
LIKE A RAGING RIVER
AS EARTH ERUPTS IN VIOLENCE.
EARTH IS ANGRY
THRUSTING ITS FISTS UP
BANGING THEM
LOUDLY AND VIOLENTLY.
THEN ... SILENCE.
EARTH'S TANTRUM OVER.
ALL IS CALM.

SATURDAY, 11 SEPTEMBER

It's been a week now since the big earthquake but it feels like forever. I went to Laura's today and we spent most of the time just talking about the earthquakes. Her house has huge cracks in the walls, and the driveway is cracked from one end to the other. On the floor in the corner of her bedroom, a crack sneaks up the wall all the way to the ceiling. Her Dad says it's safe, but Laura told me it creeps her out. It creeps me out too.

We didn't do anything except talk. When I got home, Mum was waiting for me, smiling. Dusty has come home! She looked really thin but I just picked her up and hugged her real tight. Tessa and I both cried. We were so happy to see her. I don't know where she's been, but she's back – and I am NEVER going to let her out of my sight again!

SUNDAY, 12 SEPTEMBER

Today we all piled into Dad's car and went over to Aunty Beth's place. It's like a different world there. The roads are all bumpy with cracks and holes in them. The cul-de-sac they live in is now all messy and grey. There's a massive crack across their drive and across the road where the ground has opened up. Some of the people have moved out already, as the houses aren't safe to live in. They still don't have power or water so Aunty Beth just collected more clothes and things she needs. We got out the big rubbish bags and threw out all the food from her fridge, freezer and cupboards. There was a lot of rotten food. Dad and Uncle Dave dug a hole in the garden behind the shed and trellis so that when Aunty Beth and Uncle Dave do come back, when the power is on, they will at least have a toilet. Ugh! I dragged some of the garden pots and stuck them by the trellis. I reckon if you have to wee outside in a makeshift loo then at least it should look nice.

Their lawn and drive was covered in liquefaction – horrible, thick, grey and wet. We spent hours digging it up and piling it on the side of the road. It's gross, heavy stuff. Some of the remaining neighbours came out and helped shovel too, even though they had been digging their own mountains of the stuff. The one nice thing about this earthquake is that everyone cares about everyone else and wants to help out.

The house will be liveable if they get power back on, but no one knows when that will happen. Mayor Bob Parker keeps telling everyone they are doing all they can, but it's a huge job.

MONDAY, 13 SEPTEMBER

Yahoo! Back to school today. It feels like it has been forever. All we did was talk about the earthquake. And we had a practice earthquake drill where we all had to get under our desks and pretend to be turtles. We always had fire drills before and even though we knew about earthquake drills we didn't practise them much. I don't think we really need to practise now, even, as we have already learned how to be turtles and protect ourselves.

The library was a mess – books scattered everywhere – but the teacher aides helped the librarian put it all back. The classrooms weren't damaged and the teachers had been in and picked up all the things that had fallen over, so we could get straight back to class work. Our school was really lucky. We even had choir practice at lunchtime, but we didn't get very far as Miss Finch wanted to hear everyone's stories about the earthquake and how it affected us.

Laura and I didn't get a chance to sing but Zoe and Bettina did, and they were good. Really good. I wouldn't mind if Zoe wasn't so bossy and up herself. She thinks she's better than everyone else.

THURSDAY, 16 SEPTEMBER

When I got home from school today, Mum had made the kitchen into a makeshift hairdressing salon. All the shampoos, towels, brushes and things were spread over the table.

"If I've lost my job in town then I can cut hair from home. No point in feeling sorry for myself," she said.

It was good to see Mum smile again. She has made and photocopied some flyers, letting people know where they can get their hair cut, so we went for a walk before dinner and put them in people's letterboxes. Jackson complained the whole time but Dad was still at work and Tessa was at her friend's place so we had to take him. I don't know how there is any room for a salon as we still have three extras staying with us. The big news of today was that mayor said the state of emergency is over. So hopefully that means things are going to get better now.

FRIDAY, 17 SEPTEMBER

Aunty Beth and Uncle Dave moved back to their place today. They have power now, although it comes and goes a bit. They will still shower here as their water pressure is pretty bad, with often no water at all. At least we won't have to climb over all their stuff in the lounge any more. Gran is still staying with us, but Dad says she might go to Invercargill to stay with her sister for a couple of weeks while the aftershocks keep happening.

SATURDAY, 18 SEPTEMBER

I can't believe it! We all went out to the mall today and Mum and Dad bought me a cell phone! Awesome! A real live cell phone – just for me. Tessa was so mad, and kept saying how I'm spoiled and that I should have to wait until I'm 13 like she did – and then she stuck her tongue out at me. I did the same and then we both got the giggles when this old man saw us and gave us a dirty look.

The phone isn't fancy, in fact it doesn't do a lot really, and I am not allowed to make calls unless it's for an emergency, but I am so excited. I'm also only allowed to text for proper things and not just chatting to Laura. Mum and Dad said I needed one in case of emergency because of the earthquakes. If I have a phone then they can get hold of me if I am at school. I'm not to show it around at school as the teachers don't like us having them (even though heaps of kids do) and it could get stolen. I still can't believe it. I gave them both big hugs and everything felt normal for the first time in ages.

SUNDAY, 19 SEPTEMBER

Tessa was nicer today. She even helped me with the phone and showed me how to use it. She is so fast at texting and I'm like an old lady. Slow as! But I'm getting faster. I texted Laura a bit until Mum caught me and told me she would take the phone off me if I didn't stop.

MONDAY, 20 SEPTEMBER

It is 3 o'clock in the morning and I am using my torch to write this. I don't want to wake anyone up but I can't sleep. Every time I close my eyes I hear the roaring, rumbling sound of earthquakes in my head. It's like a film going over and over in my head and I get scared all over again. I just want to sleep!

THURSDAY, 23 SEPTEMBER

I stuffed up at choir today and Laura got mad. I do know the words but I just forgot them today. Probably because I'm really, really tired. No one sleeps because we get woken up several times a night from the aftershocks. Laura told me to concentrate and I yelled at her that I was trying to and she glared at me. I should have said sorry but I got mad too, especially when Zoe grinned at me after she and Bettina were told how well they did. Miss Finch said no one would be doing a duet for this term's final assembly. Mr Thompson, the principal, would have too many things to talk about because of the earthquakes, so there wouldn't be time. We would just be singing the song the whole choir had practised. I guess at least we will still get to sing. Maybe next term we will get another chance for the duet.

FRIDAY, 24 SEPTEMBER

Yippee! End of Term 3! We are now officially on holiday – no school for two weeks. Gran flew down to Invercargill today. With Mum doing hairdressing, and us kids on holiday, Gran says she's better off away from the noise and mess and, of course, the aftershocks. I've got my room back, which is great – I don't have to share with Jackson any more. It scares me to watch Jackson sleep. He looks so small and frightened. He doesn't scream any more when the ground shakes. Instead he just kind of whimpers, a bit like a dog in the pound, all lost and lonely. I do give him lots of hugs but I can't make it better because no one knows what will happen next or when the shakes will stop.

SATURDAY, 25 SEPTEMBER

Dad took the day off work today and we drove around the city. Wow! Sydenham is really bad. So is Kaiapoi. There are still piles of liquefaction everywhere. We saw the clock tower on the Science Alive building – it had stopped at exactly 4.35 a.m. when the earthquake struck. Spooky. I took a photo for my scrapbook.

Many of the shops in town are still cordoned off, with soldiers on guard. Jackson loved that. He couldn't stop talking about the soldiers and the big tanks all day. Even at dinnertime he was still going on about them. Aunty Beth and Uncle Dave were here too so they could have showers and do their washing. I would hate not having a hot shower. They are still using the toilet they dug in their garden. I am so glad we live where we do here in Linwood.

SUNDAY, 27 SEPTEMBER

Laura came for a sleepover today and we made cupcakes so Dad could take them in for the men at his work. He works for City Care and says the job is massive and dirty. He says they're only doing temporary fixes on most of the holes as there just isn't time to do them properly. "A good rain will soak through the holes and make them sink again but they'll all get fixed properly one day." We think the job they have to do is pretty disgusting, especially as heaps of sewer pipes have broken and we just wanted to say 'thanks' so that's why we made the cupcakes. Mind you, by the time we ate some of them, there weren't too many left.

MONDAY, 28 SEPTEMBER

Jackson and I spent the day watching DVDs in Mum and Dad's bedroom. It's Gran's TV as Mum's bedroom one smashed when it fell off its stand in the earthquake. Mum had a few clients today so we stayed out of the way. Most days she doesn't have many clients, but as lots of kids get their hair cut in the holidays, it's a busier time for her. It's stink for us though. We can't go anywhere if she has to work. Tessa gets to go out with her friends or to babysit the kids down the road, but I'm stuck with an annoying 5-year-old.

SUNDAY, 3 OCTOBER

We had a barbecue at Aunty Beth's for her birthday. I was allowed to bring Laura, which was good as Jackson has been a pain all week and Laura is much better company. I showed her all the cracks and broken bits around the house. After lunch we did a practice performance for everyone. They all clapped, even Tessa (although it was only one-handed, on her knee, as she was busy texting with the other). Uncle Dave stomped his feet and cheered. He reckoned we were awesome. I don't know about awesome but I think we did better than we have in a while. It just felt right.

TUESDAY, 5 OCTOBER

Last night we had another great big aftershock. It was a magnitude 5.1. I hate it so much. The noise is deafening. You hear the rumble and roar first and you just know something horrible is going to happen. Then, when it starts, you never know when it's going to stop. Or if it *will* stop! I know it will, but at the time it just feels like it will go on and on forever. Dusty hates it too, and she hides under my bed for ages after each big one.

WEDNESDAY, 6 OCTOBER

In *The Press* today it said we have had 1439 aftershocks. Wow! **We have lived through over a thousand aftershocks!!!** No wonder we are all grumpy and tired. That's amazing.

I never used to read *The Press* much, except once a week when I had current events homework for school, but now I read it every day. It can be kind of scary reading what has been happening around us, and seeing photos of the damage. It is kind of like ... I don't want to look but I have to.

FRIDAY, 8 OCTOBER

I went to Laura's today. I still don't like being in her bedroom – the cracks freak me out. At least most of the damage to our house is on the roof and chimney, and we can't see it from inside.

We messed around doing stupid stuff. It was nice being away from Tessa and Jackson. Her mum took us out to Orana Park. It made me think about how scary it must be for the animals. They don't understand why everything shakes all the time. I think I prefer being at school these days – it makes it easier if we are all together. It was a good day though. We watched DVDs of *Glee* again until I had to go home.

MONDAY, 11 OCTOBER

So good to be back at school. Even Miss Higgins was okay and she didn't give us any homework.

Miss Finch called a meeting for the entire choir at morning tea time. She told us auditions for the final Term 4 assembly will be next week and we had better be prepared. I caught Zoe and Bettina looking at me. So smug! I bet they think the duet is theirs already. Well, they haven't heard Laura and me. I reckon we deserve it, with all the practise we did in the holidays.

MONDAY, 18 OCTOBER

I haven't written much lately as Laura and I have been singing all week, every chance we could get. I couldn't believe what happened today at choir! Zoe and Bettina sang their duet and they were sooo good. I felt a bit jealous, I have to admit. I didn't want them to be good but they were. I just know Miss Finch will give it to them. Anyway, then I let my nerves get to me and I almost ran out of breath. I didn't, thank goodness, but I knew I could have done better. So did Laura. She wasn't mad, but I think she was disappointed in me.

Miss Finch announced to the whole choir which songs we would be doing for the end of year concert, and then she asked Zoe, Bettina, Laura and me to stay behind. And then … she said we were *all* good and she couldn't decide who should do the duet so we would do TWO DUETS. Zoe glared at me again. She'd better watch out, or one day her face will stay that way. But I don't care … **Laura and I are going to do a duet in the final assembly!** It will be our last ever assembly at this school, so it's kind of cool.

TUESDAY, 19 OCTOBER

After school today, Mum, Jackson and I went over to Gran's and tidied up the house. She's coming home tomorrow, back to her own house. I put some flowers in her bedroom but the house still smells kind of musty. Her house is on a bus route and the bus stop is just next door. I got a massive fright when a bus rumbled up the road. I thought we were going to have another aftershock. Jackson was staring at me too. He wasn't sure either. It's funny, but before the earthquake, noises never worried me. Now I'm aware of every sound, and every movement. Weird, but not in a good way.

SUNDAY, 24 OCTOBER

Mum and Dad made us spend half the morning making a list of all the things we need for an emergency kit. It was a long list. Mum even wants us each to have our own backpack filled with spare clothes and a sleeping bag in the corner of the wardrobe so we can grab it in an emergency.

"You're going a bit overboard, aren't you?" Dad said.

"You never know when we're going to have the big one," she said.

"We've already had the big one!" Tessa said. Then everyone started arguing. Jackson got scared all over again and it was just horrible. Everyone is so jumpy and moody. I hate it.

Anyway, we went out and bought heaps of things and made up a kit in a big plastic container. It had so much stuff in it that even Dad complained how heavy it was. It feels really strange knowing that in the hall closet we have a kit full of food and bandages, radios and candles, batteries and bottles of water, just so we can grab it in case of emergency. We keep our own torches by our bed. I agree with Tessa and reckon that we've already had the biggest one we'll ever have. I wish it hadn't happened, but it did ... and it makes me feel nervous sometimes.

SATURDAY, 30 OCTOBER

Not much happening lately. I don't even get to hang out with Laura as she is in Timaru for the weekend with her cousins. We haven't had a chance to sing much either. I know the words off by heart now. I sing in the shower real loud until Tessa bangs on the door complaining. It's just because she can't sing. I think she enjoys complaining. Like, it's almost a hobby or something.

MONDAY, 1 NOVEMBER

My lunch went missing from my backpack today. I know it was there at morning tea time because after I got my apple out I put the rest of my lunch back in my schoolbag. I looked everywhere for my lunchbox and then finally found it in the rubbish bin. It was all tipped out so there was no way I could eat it. I bet it was Zoe who dumped it there. She was the only one in the cloakroom before lunch. She was let out of class first because she was on lunchtime reception duty in the office. No one else had the chance and no one else would do that. At least, I don't think anyone else would be that mean. If I tell the teacher she will just say Zoe wouldn't do that.

Zoe, Zoe, Zoe. Perfect little Miss Zoe! She might be able to fool everyone else but she doesn't fool me. Not for one minute. I know it was her, and one day I will prove that she is nothing more than a big mean bully. Laura gave me one of her sandwiches so I didn't go completely hungry. I told Tessa about it and she said I had no proof and it could have been anyone, but I think she might believe me, just a little bit.

FRIDAY, 12 NOVEMBER

It's the Canterbury A & P Show today, so no school. Yeah! Dad had the day off too, so here we are at Hanmer Springs for the night. We spent ages in the hot pools. Tessa and I looked like wrinkled old prunes when we got out. We had fish and chips afterwards. The fish and chips here are so good. I love the lemon pepper they sprinkle on them.

We brought a pile of DVDs from home to watch. Dad said we could bring anything except *Glee*. He doesn't know what he's missing. It was actually kind of cool to hang out together as a family. It feels like ages since we've done that. Tessa was okay – not too bossy. The place we are staying at is pretty basic and we had to bring our own sleeping bags. Tessa and I stayed up almost all night watching movies. Jackson fell asleep early. I don't know how he slept through the noise of the TV. Maybe being away from Christchurch is good for him. I know it is good for me. I haven't felt any shakes today and it is such a good feeling.

SATURDAY, 13 NOVEMBER

We all climbed Conical Hill after lunch. It was hard going in places and all zig-zaggy at the top but the views were great. I took photos for my scrapbook. Tessa whinged of course. On the way up I saw a fantail. It kept flitting about just in front of us as if it was leading us up the hill. I love the little peep-peep sound they make. I hardly ever see them in the city so it was kind of special. Tessa thought so too, even if she pretended it wasn't. Sometimes she can be so annoying trying to act all grown up. All the way home she kept poking me. Dad's car is definitely too small for us all to fit in, especially with Jackson's car seat. In the end Dad got so sick of us fighting he stopped the car and moved Jackson in between us. Jackson then started singing some stupid song, which annoyed everyone. By the time we got home, I just wanted to go to my room and blob out, but Dad made Tessa and me wash the car ... which of course ended up in a water fight. She got me good ... but I will get her back next time!

SUNDAY, 14 NOVEMBER

At about 1.30 this morning we all woke up to another horrible shake. It's not fair. I just want to forget about them. When we go away we can forget, but the minute we come back it all starts again. We always check on the Internet to see what magnitude the aftershocks are and how deep they. The shallow ones are the worst. We can even see where they are strongest. Sometimes they are centred over in Darfield, or out west, and other times it is in the east and close by.

WEDNESDAY, 17 NOVEMBER

I came home from school today and heard Mum talking to someone on the phone. She was arguing about the roof and chimney and her car. It must've been the insurance company. Or it could have been EQC. Everyone moans about the Earthquake Commission. No one likes dealing with them, but Mum was really cross and loud. She never gets cross on the phone. I pretended I didn't hear her and went straight to my room. I tried doing my homework but couldn't really concentrate. I texted Laura, which filled in some time until dinner. I really didn't want to go in to the lounge while Mum was in such a bad mood.

SATURDAY, 20 NOVEMBER

I went to Laura's early today as her Mum was taking us to a school fair. I bought a pile of junk at the fair – magazines, craft stuff for my scrapbooking, ribbons and buttons. I ate far too much candyfloss and coconut ice. The Russian fudge was a bit sugary but for only $1.00 a bag it was okay. I bought a pot plant for Mum, seeing as the fallen chimney smashed the ones at the back door during the earthquake.

I really think I ate too much junk at the fair coz I don't feel too good now. I'm going to bed.

TUESDAY, 23 NOVEMBER

Choir was so cool. It was brilliant! Miss Finch had some ex-pupils from our school come in at lunchtime and sing us a song they were doing for their school production. They were Year 10s and very good. They know Tessa as they all go to Avonside Girls' High, where she goes. I don't know how they know her as Tessa doesn't sing. She's really good at swimming though. Maybe they swim too. I sure hope Zoe won't go to Avonside – it's bad enough that we're going to the same intermediate next year. I would hate it at the same high school. Even Zoe was impressed with these girls. I could tell by the look in her face. She was too busy watching them to spend any time annoying me. So yeah! It was a good day.

WEDNESDAY, 1 DECEMBER

Only 17 more days of school until the Christmas holidays. Can't wait. Actually it feels a bit strange. I don't know if I am excited or sad. I can't wait for intermediate and all the different things I can do there but I feel sad to be leaving primary school. I've been here for six years and made lots of friends. I'll even miss some of the teachers. Some kids are going to a different intermediate so I won't see them but most of us are going to the same one. Even Zoe and Bettina are going to the same one as me.

SATURDAY, 4 DECEMBER

Mum drove me to Aunty Beth's so I could do odd jobs to make money to buy Christmas presents. Aunty Beth said there wasn't much point in doing too much as the house will probably be demolished. The land underneath it is so bad that nothing can be rebuilt on it.

I love her house. It's new and warm and just over the back fence is the Wetlands. We nearly always go for a walk there when we go to Aunty Beth's. I love watching the black swans gliding over the water. Their necks are so long and they curve like question marks. My favourite birds are the pukeko. They are so cheeky! They just walk along in front of me and whenever I go to take a photo, they run off almost like they are laughing at me. It's really sad that the land here is ruined. I wonder what will happen to all the birds.

MONDAY, 6 DECEMBER

Today in class we planned a shared lunch for the last week of term. It has to be on Thursday the second to last day as the last day is just really for the final assembly and to wish everyone a happy Christmas. Laura and I are going to make cupcakes with red and green icing for Christmas.

SUNDAY, 12 DECEMBER

I did heaps of jobs at Gran's today to earn money for Christmas. I washed dishes and vacuumed the house, washed floors and did dusting. Then Mum got mad at me. She said I should be doing these things for Gran anyway, without asking for money, but Gran had already agreed. It was even her idea. Tessa earns money babysitting the little kids down the road from us so she's okay, but I don't have a job and Mum won't let me get a paper round. She says there are too many dogs and idiots out there. So just how am I supposed to earn money? It is so annoying. Sometimes Dad gives me money for helping him in the garden. Mum says because they lost things in the earthquake that needed replacing and because the insurance hasn't paid out, Christmas won't be much this year. She said, "We can go shopping on Boxing Day when all the sales are on." I guess that will be good.

TUESDAY, 14 DECEMBER

Jackson has been so excited all day. He hung around me and Laura at lunchtime and showed us a book he was given in class. All the year one and two kids in Christchurch were given a picture book about a cat in an earthquake. It is called *Quaky Cat* and it's quite cute. It's about a cat getting lost after a big quake and then finding its way home. It has pictures of broken houses and the cat even has tears. Animals do get frightened too. I know, because Dusty did. She got so scared she ran away. Then she took ages to come home again. Mum, Tessa and I have all read the book to Jackson. I think it's his new favourite book. Dad is reading it to him now. I can hear his voice in Jackson's room. I remember when Dad used to read to me too when I was younger. It was a nice feeling.

WEDNESDAY, 15 DECEMBER

Laura and I made cupcakes after school today. We smeared red icing over the top of them and then made little green leaves to look like holly. They looked a bit weird but they'll do. Laura stayed for tea so we had one last practice for Friday's assembly. And ate some of the cupcakes too.

THURSDAY, 16 DECEMBER

The shared lunch was cool. We ate so much stuff – cakes, chocolate, cheerios – and drank so much fizzy drink that we were all crazy stupid and hyper all afternoon. Laura and I were so mad though. Zoe (ugh, I hate that name) made Christmas cupcakes and they had little snowmen on top. She knew Laura and I were doing cupcakes and she was supposed to bring lolly cake, but she did cupcakes just to outdo us. Tessa reckoned I was just jealous because they were better than ours. I thought Tessa would've been on my side. Sisters! Who needs them?

FRIDAY, 17 DECEMBER
Last day of term and my last day at primary school – ever!

I was too excited to eat breakfast this morning but Mum made me eat a piece of toast. She said, in her very serious voice meant to make a point, "Maddy, you will not leave this house until you have eaten something."

So I ate the stupid toast, but it sat in my stomach for ages.

Today felt really weird. I was excited, but also sad about leaving. It feels safe here. My friends are here and everything I've ever known has been at this school. But on the other hand, I can't wait for intermediate.

Assembly was awesome. I remembered to take a deep breath before Laura and I started our song and it must have gone well because everyone clapped heaps. I loved it. I loved being up there in front of the whole school just singing my heart out. It felt so good. It felt just right! Zoe and Bettina sang really well too and I actually liked it. I would never ever let them know that though. The kapa haka group did a farewell to all us Year 6s and the teachers who were leaving. That was when some of us started crying. Well, just a wee bit. Mum and Dad both came to assembly, which was cool.

All of us seniors had made our own graduation hats – all basically the same, with black cardboard and a flat top, but we got to add things on top which were special

55

to us. Lots of the boys in my class used Lego. Ben had plastic bugs and spiders. Gross! I had some song sheets which I creased into a fan and stuck that on top with the cover of the *Glee* DVD. That's me. Music all the way! Laura's was good too with cupcake cut-outs and lollies spread out. I hope she didn't use glue to hold them on or she won't be able to eat them later.

Fun day!

SUNDAY, 19 DECEMBER

We all went Christmas shopping today at Riccarton Mall. Dad's still working six days a week so we had to wait until Sunday to go. Mum hasn't got a new car yet as she is still arguing with the insurance people, so we can only do things in Dad's car. We also bought some stuff for the Salvation Army boxes. A lot of people still have to go to the toilet outside and their houses are still not fixed and I feel so bad for them. I'd hate to spend Christmas in a broken home. I hope no one (mostly that means you, Tessa) reads my diary in case they find out what I bought them.

MONDAY, 20 DECEMBER

Mum had a heap of people wanting their hair cut today. She was so busy, we were stuck in our bedrooms all day.

Mum said it was a good thing and I shouldn't complain. "Haircuts mean money, Maddy," she said.

After dinner I wrapped up my gifts for everyone. I got Tessa an iTunes card, and bought Jackson a little Lego set.

I didn't have much money left for Mum and Dad so I bought them a shared gift. When the earthquake hit, some of the photo frames broke when they fell on the floor and things fell on top of them. I printed off a photo of us all and put it in a new frame. I hope they like it.

THURSDAY, 23 DECEMBER

Tessa and I made fudge and coconut ice. When it was set, we cut it up and put a few pieces of each in little cellophane bags. We did bags for Gran, Aunty Beth and Uncle Dave, and Mrs Williams next door. She's been back a while and I know she will go to her son's over Christmas, but she is really kind and I like her a lot. Tessa wanted some for her friends and the family she babysits for, too. It was nice for us to do something together. Thank goodness Jackson was playing at a friend's house all day. He would've just got in the way if he was here. We tied the bags up with Christmas ribbon and they looked cool. We made our own cards as well.

Tessa and I caught the bus in to South City and dropped off the toys we got for the Salvation Army Christmas appeal. The radio station collects them each year from the middle of the mall and we always drop off something, but this year we added extra things. This year Christmas will be hard for some people. Then Tessa and I had sushi and a drink while we waited for the bus to go home.

It was an awesome day!

SATURDAY, 25 DECEMBER
Christmas Day

I woke up early this morning. Real early, but I sure wasn't going to be first up. Tessa would give me a hard time if I was. So I just lay there, waiting for Jackson to get up. I heard him get out of bed just before seven so I got up too and made him toast. By then everyone was up.

Jackson was so excited. He ripped into his presents so fast he almost missed one. Mum and Dad gave him Lego too, so he was really happy. Tessa unwrapped hers so slowly and neatly it was annoying. I know she just wanted to rip into them. She got mostly vouchers and some perfume. I got vouchers too. Tessa gave me a new diary for next year. It has awesome borders and a special box to keep it in. It's cool.

Aunty Beth and Uncle Dave came over for lunch and they picked up Gran on the way. We had roast chicken, roast vegetables, garlic bread and salads. So much food. Then, when I couldn't fit any more in, we had pudding – pavlova with strawberries, kiwifruit and heaps of cream. Jackson ended up with so much cream over his face he looked like a zombie foaming at the mouth! He didn't care – he just licked all the cream off with his tongue. Boys are so gross.

After lunch, we all just blobbed out. Mum wanted to go for a walk but nobody else did, so she gave up and we ended up watching Christmas movies on TV instead. I love Christmas. Everyone is so nice and happy.

Laura rang me – she got heaps of things but she said the best was a new iPod. I might see her tomorrow when we get back from the Boxing Day sales. I can't wait. I love spending vouchers.

SUNDAY, 26 DECEMBER
Boxing Day

We had breakfast early this morning because none of us got much sleep after being woken just after 2 a.m. by another big aftershock. Still hate them. The good thing was, it meant we were all up and ready to go to the Boxing Day sales nice and early! The shops are always so crowded on Boxing Day and you have to get to the malls early or you just won't get a park. Dad stayed home. He said he wanted to stay away from the crowds and shops and enjoy some quiet time at home. I know he has been working lots of extra days to help with the roads so I didn't mind that he didn't come shopping.

The rest of us got to South City mall just before ten o'clock. That was going to be our first stop, and then we would walk into town. It was already busy and I think lots of people must have come in and had breakfast in the food court just so they could be first in the doors when the sales started. Some people are so rude, pushing to get inside the shops to see what's going cheap. And that was just the beginning of the day …

I still get the shakes when I think about what happened next. We were in Glassons looking at some tops at about 10.30 when it happened all over again. The noise came first and we all froze. We knew what was coming next. All the coat hangers and clothes started banging together and the rumble was so loud I could hear it over all the people talking and walking in the mall. The glass windows were rattling and I saw a massive crack shoot right across the glass of the side plate-glass window, all the way to the top. It was freaky to be in there with so much noise and shaking. Jackson grabbed hold of Mum and Tessa actually grabbed me by the arm.

Mum just said, loudly, "C'mon, we're out of here." As she spoke, the shop people also asked us all to leave and assemble in the car park. Not that we needed to be told. We were getting out of there as fast as we could. The noise of everyone talking and hurrying outside was strange – it sounded sort of buzzy and frantic.

Mum got a call from Dad almost straight away and then

Tessa and I both got texts at the same time. I don't know who hers was from but mine was from Laura, wanting to know if I was okay. Everyone just wants to make sure everyone is okay. I am so glad I have my phone. I texted back that I was okay but scared. She texted back – same!

When we got to the car it took ages to get out. Everyone was trying to leave at the same time. The traffic lights weren't working, so that meant the power was out again somewhere – which made it even harder to get home. None of the cars driving down Durham Street would stop to let us out of the mall car park. I think everyone in town was trying to escape the same way as us, and traffic was at a standstill. Sort of like watching a movie in slow motion. Horrible. I felt so mad! I just want it to stop happening. We can't even go shopping without stupid aftershocks.

When we did get home, Dad gave us all a hug. It felt so good. I hate being freaked out.

On the news tonight they said that the earthquake was a 4.9 and centred in Sydenham. That's really close to South City, which is why we felt it so strong – we were really close. They said on the news it was shallow and the way it shook made it a really damaging one. Shoppers in town had concrete and bricks and broken glass fall around them. Aunty Beth rang Mum, crying on the phone because they had more liquefaction, all over their street and lawns and drive. We are going over tomorrow to help dig it up.

Desna Wallace

I think my brain is numb. I just want to go to sleep and forget about the quakes. I am going to sleep in my clothes again tonight. Just in case. Boxing Day was supposed to have been so much fun. Instead it was another scary day.

MONDAY, 27 DECEMBER

I woke up this morning with my torch by my head. I must have fallen asleep with it in my hand. I don't want to go anywhere today. I don't even want to read. I just want to watch DVDs and stay inside.

But of course I didn't get to do that. We all went to Aunty Beth's and helped her and Uncle Dave dig up liquefaction. I can't believe how much mess there is. It is all grey and thick and yucky. It took ages but most of the people still left in the street were out doing the same thing. Everyone is sick of the earthquakes. Me too.

FRIDAY, 31 DECEMBER
New Year's Eve

Laura came over for lunch and we just mucked about. I don't think she likes her house much. I got the feeling the Boxing Day aftershock really scared her but she won't say much. Jackson was a pain. Mum had a couple of clients who wanted their hair done for New Year's Eve parties and Tessa was at a friend's place so Laura and I got stuck keeping an eye on Jackson. Everything we did, he wanted to do too. He promised us he would leave us alone if we read him a few books. So we did but he was still a pain.

Laura was allowed to sleep over so we stayed up until after midnight. Mum, Dad, Aunty Beth, Uncle Dave and us kids all sang Auld Lang Syne at midnight. Dad really shouldn't sing – he is so out of tune and then he just sings louder if we say anything. It was a pretty good night. Laura and I talked for ages. I don't remember what time we fell asleep but it was really late. Dad banged on the door at 2 a.m. and told us to settle down. We whispered for a while after that but not too long.

SATURDAY, 1 JANUARY 2011

We didn't get up until after 10.30 today. Then we hung around in our pyjamas, cooking pancakes for breakfast. I don't think I will ever get the hang of cooking. I end up in such a mess no matter how hard I try not to. Laura just giggles and calls me hopeless. The pancakes must have tasted okay though, because everyone wanted more. After lunch we finally got dressed and watched DVDs and – yes – *Glee*. That started an argument. Dad said it really is a bit too raunchy, whatever that is! Mum said it was harmless and really all about the singing. Yay for Mum!

That cheer didn't last long. In the afternoon Tessa walked with us to Laura's house. She grumbled all the way saying she shouldn't have to babysit us. I told her straight up that I agreed. Mum has been worse since the big earthquake and just doesn't want to leave us alone. It's okay for us to walk to school and back, but not to Laura's. Go figure. She says that's because it's okay if we are walking together but that I would have to walk back by myself. But I'm eleven! She just doesn't get it.

SUNDAY, 9 JANUARY 2011

Mum, Aunty Beth, Tessa, Jackson and I went to the Arts Centre today. I love the Arts Centre. It's like a rabbit warren with nooks and crannies and hidden rooms filled to the brim with crafts and cool things. Some of the stuff they sell as antiques is just junk, I reckon, but it's still a great place. It has a wonderful atmosphere and everyone is so friendly. I really love the Fudge Cottage place. I spent too much money on walnut fudge but it was worth it. Yum!

We sat around outside listening to some of the buskers for a while. There's always someone singing or juggling or doing something strange and wonderful. Then we went on to the museum – I haven't been there for ages, so it was kind of cool looking at all the old things. I love the penny-farthing bicycle in the old street, and I absolutely LOVE the old doll's house. Everything is just so small and perfect. Jackson was so excited at the spiders and insects. Yuck! He didn't want to come home when it was time to go. He wanted to look at the spiders all over again ... and again.

When we got home, Dad had cooked dinner. Surprise – it wasn't too bad. Sausages and chips.

THURSDAY, 13 JANUARY

Jackson turns 6 today – and don't we all know it. He was up so early I think he beat the birds. After lunch he had a few friends over for a pirate party. The kids all wore pirate hats, pirate eye patches and had cutlasses and hooks for hands. They did look cute but they were noisy. I tried hiding inside, but Mum made me and Tessa supervise some of the games. We made a treasure hunt with clues and they had to search through the garden. For a prize we wrapped up chocolate bars. Mum brought out a Treasure Island cake, which did look very cool and yummy. Well, it didn't look yummy for long because I think there was more spit coming out when he blew out the birthday candles than air. But Jackson didn't care or notice. He was having such a good time.

FRIDAY, 21 JANUARY

Finally, Laura's back from her holiday in Timaru. I've missed her. We went to the movies at Hoyts in town. Tessa and her friend Rosie came too. Mum said we could only go if we all went together. I beat Tessa at air hockey again in Time Out but she won enough tickets on the other games to get a prize. I don't care, as long as I can beat her at something.

WEDNESDAY, 26 JANUARY

Today we went shopping at Eastgate Mall and bought all our stationery for school. It's hard to believe but next week I will be at intermediate. We had heaps more things to buy than we had to have for primary school. At home after I unpacked all my new stuff and named it all, it suddenly hit me how much extra work I'm going to have to do. Scary thought really. I just hope I end up in the same class as Laura.

WEDNESDAY, 2 FEBRUARY

Yes!!! Laura and I are in the same class. Awesome! The downside is that both Zoe and Bettina are in the same class too but I think I can cope with that, knowing Laura is with me. School is amazing. Our form teacher is Mr Hayes and so far he seems okay. We get split up for some of our subjects. Next week we get to choose all the options we want to do, like cooking. Maybe we'll get to make cupcakes and I can learn to bake them without leaving such a mess. And I can't wait to audition for choir (even if I am mega nervous). We already have camp booked for the end of February out at Woodend. It's our getting-to-know-one-another camp.

I LOVE MY NEW SCHOOL!!!

Friday, 11 February

There are big sales on everywhere today and all weekend. The malls have called it the Try Again Boxing Day Sale after the big aftershock on the real Boxing Day ruined it for everyone. We did go to the mall for dinner and a bit of a spend-up. I still had some mall vouchers and some money from doing odd jobs, and Dad gave me some extra money after I begged and pleaded with him to help me buy a new camera. My old one is munted. I told him I could use it at school camp and other school things. He gave me one of his I-know-when-I'm-being-played-Maddy looks but he gave in and I bought a new digital camera with more megapixels than my old one. It's awesome. I've already taken heaps of photos.

Jackson bought more Lego, but that's no surprise. He loves the stuff. I do too, really, so we spent time tonight building Lego villages.

SATURDAY, 12 FEBRUARY

Mum bought a new car today. It's kind of a beat-up old thing, but it goes well and is much better than her old one that was damaged from the earthquake. She's been smiling all day. It's worth less than her other one but the insurance company said her other car wasn't worth much. I think Mum just got sick of arguing with them. Tessa kept hassling Mum, reminding her that in April it will be her birthday and she will be 15 – old enough to learn to drive. Mum just shook her head and said, "Not in my new car!" and Dad shook his head and said, "Not in my car either."

Tessa stormed off, saying, "How am I ever going to learn if you don't let me use your car?"

"Buy your own," said Dad.

I think Tessa has quite a bit of money in the bank from her babysitting. She's pretty good at saving and she might even have enough for her own car already. I might buy her the Road Code for her birthday.

THURSDAY, 17 FEBRUARY

Yes! Yes! Yes! Laura and I got into the choir. The audition was pretty intense but we made it. So did Zoe and Bettina but that's okay. I can live with that. Next week we're going to choose songs and do a few assembly performances later in the term. I love this school. It's so good I can't wait for next week.

 # TUESDAY, 22 FEBRUARY

The WORST day EVER, EVER, EVER!

I can't believe this has happened again.

We've had another massive earthquake – but this time so much worse.

I keep crying. I can't stop.

At 12.51 p.m., right in the middle of lunchtime, everything began shaking, rattling and going crazy. The rumbling, growling, angry earth was SO LOUD we all just knew straight away this was going to be big – much bigger than anything we'd seen before.

Laura and I were in the library when the books started falling off the shelves and the shelves began moving across the room. The librarian just yelled at us to do the turtle and get down and away from the glass windows. Even from inside the library I could hear kids screaming. The sound of hundreds of kids screaming and running, absolutely terrified, is stuck in my head. All around us things were falling and crashing everywhere and it felt so much worse than before. It just seemed to go on and on and on.

When it stopped we ran outside and onto the courts where we lined up in our fire drill areas. Laura and I grabbed hold of each other and I know she was as scared as me. I was worried about Jackson. I know how much he hates aftershocks. I was worried about Tessa too. She was off school as most of her teachers were going to a union meeting in town. Tessa and Mum would be alone in the house. I just wanted to be at home with my family, but no one was allowed to leave until their parents came to get them. We could see the traffic was already backed up and not moving. It could take a long time for Dad or Mum to get here. There was no power so the traffic lights would be out too.

The teachers looked really scared too. They kept telling us everything would be okay, but they couldn't hide the truth. We knew this was bad. I tried texting Mum and Dad but I couldn't get any reception. The teachers were trying to text too and looking at each other, some of them were trying not to cry but you could see they were just as scared as us.

It isn't fair that this has happened to us – again.

One of the teachers went out to her car and listened on the radio for any information she could get. She came back and we overheard her tell the other teachers that the radio stations were down and the only news was coming through from stations outside Christchurch.

Some parents ran into the school, crying. It was awful. If grown-ups were crying like that, it had to be bad. I know the teachers didn't want us to hear anything but we couldn't help hearing stuff from people who came into the school talking about it. Someone said that lots of people had died, and a bus was completely crushed. I heard someone say that town was gone. It sounded so bad I started crying again.

People dead! I don't want to believe it. It has to be wrong. It just can't be true. This sort of thing doesn't happen here. It happens overseas but not here. We watch it on TV in other countries. Please don't let it be true! Not in my town. Not in my city. I'm so glad Laura was with me. I know I wouldn't have coped on my own.

Lots of parents had come and taken their kids but there was still no sign of Mum. I knew she would go to Jackson first, and that was right, but when there were only a few of us left we had another big aftershock. The whole tennis court started shuddering and heaving upwards. The ground moved in waves, surging forwards, up and down, over and over, like we were on a rollercoaster. As the ground moved up and down, so did we. We couldn't do anything to stop it. It is NOT normal to see the ground move like that. I was so scared – totally freaked out. I just wanted to be home, safe with Mum and Dad.

Finally, Mum arrived, with Jackson and Tessa. They all looked terrified and I was trying to be brave but as soon as I saw them I cried. We were allowed to take Laura with us. Somehow Mum had got a text from Laura's dad asking us to look after her.

They had walked to the school as it was quicker and safer than driving, even if it took ages. Cars were stuck in traffic and people were driving over footpaths just trying to get home. As we got closer to home there was liquefaction in some streets. Trying to walk through it is like stomping through thick mud. We were lucky and only had a little bit to get through, but some cars got stuck in it and had been abandoned. I think the road underneath had given way and left big holes. There were constant sounds of alarms going off and ambulances and fire engines speeding through the streets – or at least trying to. There were so many cars blocking the way, they were having a tough job getting through. I've never heard anything like it before in my life.

Mum wouldn't tell us about anything she had heard. She said, "Let's just get home." Jackson pushed his way between Mum and me and held our hands. I could feel how little his hand was and how tight he held on. I knew I had to stay strong then, for Jackson, but I grabbed Laura's hand and she grabbed Tessa's and that's how we walked home, hand in hand, through broken streets on the worst day ever.

I couldn't believe the mess when we got home! There was liquefaction in the garden in places and along the road. Inside, it looked like a disaster. Ha, that almost made me laugh – of course it *was* a disaster. A massive earthquake. Once again our city has been shaken so violently that buildings have fallen down. But this time, people have died. All through the house was mess: broken glass, books, all the food and jars from the pantry. The new photo frame I gave Mum and Dad for Christmas had fallen and chipped at the edge.

I just can't believe it. Not again! Mum checked on Mrs Williams next door and found a note on the door. Her son had come and taken her away. "That's a relief," said Mum.

Dad finally got home at 7 p.m. and we all hugged each other. He just shook his head and I knew that this day was going to be the worst I would live through ever in my whole life.

Again Mum had to take photos of all the damage before we were allowed to clean anything up.

It was hard because there were so many aftershocks. Jackson wouldn't leave Mum alone. He hung on to her and followed her everywhere. At about 8 p.m. Dad made us some sandwiches, which we were eating when Laura's dad arrived. He had her sleeping bag with him and asked us to keep her for the night. Laura didn't want to stay but her Dad told her she had to. He said their house is pretty bad and he wanted her somewhere safe for the night.

Then, just after he left, Aunty Beth and Uncle Dave and Gran arrived with their bags. The house was full again.

"Isn't it great that we still have the old outdoor dunny we can put up quickly?" said Dad, trying to be funny. None of us laughed.

Dusty is missing again. I hope she is somewhere safe and warm.

From what we can gather, this earthquake was 6.3 – smaller than September's 7.1, but centred closer to Christchurch so it was more destructive. Most of the city centre has been severely damaged and many people have died. Apparently, people as far north as Tauranga and as far south as Invercargill reckon they felt it! It is the east side of the city (our side) that has had the most damage. The other side of the city is doing okay and most still have power and water. I don't care about the damage or the broken things. I don't care that our house has cracks and a wonky roof. I just care that so many people are dead.

Laura, Tessa and I are all supposed to sleep in my room, with Gran in Tessa's room and Aunty Beth and Uncle Dave on the lounge floor. In the end, we slept in the lounge, all squished up together. It felt safer that way, despite all the rumbling, growling, shaking, horrible aftershocks and no power. We slept in our clothes with torches by our pillows, ready to run if things got worse. It is so hard to sleep though when Jackson is whimpering, there are sirens going off everywhere, the adults are talking and the ground is moving.

I cried myself to sleep. Silent tears so no one would hear me. Aftershocks woke me and I found I had a soggy pillow, wet with tears.

WEDNESDAY, 23 FEBRUARY

Amazingly, the newspaper came out today! It was printed in the North Island as the Press building in town is crumbling. The photos in the paper were awful – buildings collapsing or in ruins, and photos of people running in fear for their lives. The look in their eyes is horrible. You can actually see how terrified they are.

Some people are still trapped in buildings. The mayor has declared another state of emergency and the Civil Defence and soldiers are everywhere. Special rescue dogs are searching through the rubble looking for survivors and there are special rescue teams from overseas coming to try and help find the trapped people.

It makes me feel sick and I just want to cry.

The earthquake was centred over Lyttelton way and was very shallow, which is why this side of town and the city centre suffered so much damage.

Dad went to work but the rest of us stayed home picking up all the things that had fallen and broken. I don't even know where to start in my bedroom as everything is on the floor. All the books in my bookcase fell out and the bookcase toppled on top of them. Most of the books will be okay but some have got broken spines and ripped pages. I put the books in piles in the wardrobe. I don't want to have to keep picking them up after each big shake. I think now that this is going to keep on happening, again and again.

Under a pile of books I found my old cat ornament – broken. I got it from Nana when I was born. It must have slammed up against the wall and was now smashed into pieces. Really sad. It was the only thing I had left from her. She died when I was nine. I don't want to show Dad as it was his mum's from when she was a little girl, but I don't want to throw it out either. I'll wrap it in tissue and hide it at the bottom of my sock drawer. Maybe I'll show Dad one day.

We still haven't got power or water but lucky we had some batteries in our emergency kit so we can use the little radio. Mum and Aunty Beth walked to the dairy to get bottled water but they had run out. On the radio the announcers said there will be places to go and get water soon. Actually, without water and with so many people living in the house, there is a definite smell. Body odour. It's a bit nasty not having a shower or a wash for so long.

Tessa has hardly said a thing all day. She's really quiet. Jackson whimpers and Laura and I moped around the house. The power came back on about 5.30 p.m. in time to watch the news, but it looks like news of the earthquake has been running all day.

We all watched, except Jackson. Mum told him to stay in his room but that just made him cry. He won't even go to the toilet on his own. We have to go outside with him.

The news is frightening and so sad. So many images of people covered with blood. So many ruined buildings and cars buried in bricks. Some of the cars have messages written on their doors or windows letting people know that the car has been checked and no one is trapped inside. No one knows how many people are dead yet, because so many are still missing or trapped. The mayor said the death toll could climb much higher. I hope no one I know is hurt. The hospital ran out of ambulances during the day and injured people were carried in cars and taken to makeshift emergency centres.

Gran reckons it's like a war zone. It makes me sad because she looks so scared. She looks really old all of a sudden.

Laura's dad came over tonight. He said they were going to Timaru for a while, but it would more than likely be for a long time as their house is ruined and unsafe to live in. Laura hasn't seen it yet, but he wants her to stay another night while her parents pack up some of her belongings and talk to the insurance people and EQC if they can get through on the phones.

She argued with her dad but in the end Mum took her hand and said, "Honey, you are safe with us and your dad is trying to do his best. Make the most of tonight and maybe we can all hang out telling stories to each other."

It didn't make Laura feel any better. Her face was kind of crumpled and on the verge of tears, but she did stop arguing. We certainly didn't have any kind of storytelling session. For dinner we had cheese toasties.

Laura and I slept in our clothes, snuggled up on the lounge floor, but I couldn't sleep. I kept seeing the images from the news, and the constant aftershocks are so scary because you just don't know how big they will get. And tomorrow my best friend in the whole world is going to Timaru and I don't know when she will be back. If she hasn't got a house to come back to, she might not ever come back.

I hate this earthquake and everything it has done. You know what else it's done? It's scared the birds away. I haven't heard or seen any birds since the earthquake. There is an eerie silence in the mornings, which I don't like at all.

THURSDAY, 24 FEBRUARY

The news is on almost all the time. I can't get away from it. I'm glued to the TV, too scared to turn away in case I miss something, but I'm also almost too scared to look. In a way, I don't want to know what's happening. I just want to pretend it never happened and hope it will all go away, but it is weird because I also NEED to know. I need to know what is happening to my city.

The biggest news is that the CTV building collapsed and there was a fire and so many people are trapped inside, probably dead. There's a language school on one of the floors and the foreign students are trapped in the rubble and have most probably died. It is so horrific. I keep thinking about the poor people stuck in those buildings. People who won't ever come home again. Students who won't ever go to school again. It's just too hard to understand all of what has happened in the last few days.

A lot of people are homeless and living with friends or in community centres, and heaps more have left the city altogether. I feel numb. Laura left today and I miss her already. When we had to say goodbye we both cried. Her mum has already enrolled her in a school down in Timaru so I don't think she'll be back for ages.

It's not fair! Why can't everything just go back to the way it was? No earthquakes, no broken homes and no dead people. No sirens and no helicopters and no soldiers. I agree with Gran. Christchurch does look like a war zone from what I've seen on the news on TV.

Tonight I looked at myself in Mum's bedroom mirror – but it wasn't me looking back. It was a face I didn't recognise: no smile, tired eyes and full of fear. The same fear I see in Mum's face and everyone else I know. It's like a possum caught in the headlights on a country road. But it is me. I am scared and I am tired and I am sad – and without Laura, I am lonely.

FRIDAY, 25 FEBRUARY

Today, Gran flew to Invercargill. I know I will miss her too but Mum says it's for the best. Gran will cope better away from all the chaos and we won't have to worry about her. So both Gran and Laura have left Christchurch now. I think I want to leave too. And Dusty still hasn't come home. I hope she is just hiding out, like last time. In the paper there are reports that hundreds of pets have gone missing. People have put notes up everywhere, even on Trade Me.

Tessa has been really kind today. I didn't think she would understand how bad I feel about Laura going but she does. She gets what it is like to lose your best friend. Mum says when things settle down Laura might come back and in the meantime we can email each other. It won't be the same as going to school together, or singing and spending the weekends doing things though. With Laura here I feel strong, but without her everything seems so much worse.

SATURDAY, 26 FEBRUARY

We have been told that we should try to collect rainwater if it rains. Dad and Uncle Dave draped a tarpaulin over the clothesline and folded it so if it rains the water will run down the tarpaulin into a bucket. Dad cut off the bottom end of one of the drainpipes near the corner of the house and put a bucket under that, too, to collect water if it rains. It feels like we are stuck on some island in the middle of the ocean after being shipwrecked and have to do everything we can to survive. Okay so it's not a shipwreck, but we are in survival mode just the same. It's like something you would read about, not something you'd ever expect to be living through.

Tonight when Dad read the paper, he called out to Mum. "Did you see the government's cancelled the census? Thank goodness for that. I hate the stupid things. It's just an excuse for the government to pry into our business."

Mum laughed at him and said the government had to do the census every five years to work out where best to spend its money.

"Well, they can spend it all on rebuilding Christchurch instead," he said. "And anyway, with so many people leaving the city, and others homeless and jobless, what else could they do but cancel it?"

I can't even imagine building a new Christchurch. I love it just as it is. Well, the way it was. And, anyway, where would you start? It is just too hard to think about.

SUNDAY, 27 FEBRUARY

We have water today – yahoo! It's been **days** since any of us had a shower or wash. We still have to go outside for the toilet but at least we can have a shower now. They said on the radio that we have to boil all water as it could be contaminated as lots of sewer pipes have been damaged. Some people have even had sewer pipes burst on their properties so they have liquefaction, flooding **and** sewage. Gross!

I guess I should feel lucky – and I know I am. We don't have any of that stuff floating in our back yard. Our house is okay, and although it is damaged it's only cosmetic Dad says, although the roof still needs to be repaired from the September earthquake. It's just that I don't feel very lucky or happy with so much sadness and tragedy in Christchurch.

The news gets worse all the time. More people have been added to the death list because they have found and counted their bodies.

And always the ground keeps on shaking.

MONDAY, 28 FEBRUARY

Schools are still closed and we don't know when they will re-open. Some reports say a few schools are so bad they won't open for months – or maybe not at all this year. Maybe never! I hope my school is okay, although going there without Laura won't be any fun.

When Dad came home from work today he looked so tired. He said some of the roads are completely stuffed. They are only doing patch-up repairs to make the roads safe enough to drive on. They can't fix the roads properly until the sewage and water pipes in the ground are all repaired, which means even more roads need to be dug up – and when all that is done, then they can make permanent repairs to the roads. He said Avonside Drive, where Tessa goes to school, is a mess. River Road and others in that area are so full of potholes and buckled so badly it is too dangerous to drive there. Bower Ave and parts of New Brighton have roads that you can't go down as they are so badly damaged with broken pipes and liquefaction piled high. The houses are falling down, too. He just shakes his head and says it's going to take years and years to fix Christchurch. He hasn't been into the centre of town yet as it is still only emergency workers and Civil Defence allowed in there.

"Town might be ruined but the suburbs have also been hit hard." Then he shakes his head again and says, "No wonder so many people are leaving Christchurch."

I thought of Laura and Gran and it made me feel sad all over again.

TUESDAY, 1 MARCH

What a hassle it was getting groceries today. Mum wouldn't leave us alone in the house in case there was another big aftershock, and Aunty Beth was at her house checking on it, so we had to go all the way over to Hornby with Mum. It was miles away and took forever because so many roads are damaged and closed off and so many people were doing the same thing. It was just a massive traffic jam. The supermarkets and malls on our side are all shut or damaged. We used to go to Eastgate Mall to get groceries but half of that has fallen down. St Martin's supermarket, where we also go sometimes, has been damaged and closed up too. We didn't really have a choice but to go all the way to Hornby and the supermarket there was so packed it took forever. There were lots of gaps on the shelves where they had run out of things. Everyone was buying bottled water, milk and bread. We hadn't done any shopping since before the earthquake so the trolley was full to the top with vegetables and meat and just about everything else. Mum bought heaps of hand sanitiser and disinfectant too.

"You have to be careful," she said. We can't rely on our water or sewage systems so we have to make sure we clean up even more now. We don't want to get sick on top of everything else going on."

The queues were so long that Jackson got bored – and when he gets bored he becomes this horrible, irritating monster of a brother. I think Mum felt sorry for us being cooped up in the house all the time coz she bought us chocolate, potato chips and fizzy drink and she hardly ever does that. When we got home, Aunty Beth was waiting for us with the TV on for the special news break.

We stood together at 12.51 when the whole country stood for two minutes silence to remember the quake, one week ago today. We just looked at each other and, even though we didn't cry out loud, we all had tears in our eyes. It was awful. They want us to remember those that have died and I do. But I also want to forget, like it never happened. Does that make me awful?

Later, I heard on the news that a baby had died during the earthquake when a TV fell on him. When I heard that I got real angry. I was yelling at Tessa and she stood right up in my face and shouted back at me. "It's not **my** fault. I didn't make the stupid earthquake. It just happened. Okay?" And then Mum came through and just hugged us.

"It's no one's fault," she said. "It is just a horrible, nasty, tragedy that we have to deal with. And we will deal with it. We have each other and we are safe," and she cried too. I hate seeing her cry.

When Dad got home he must've wanted to rush back out again with all of us so tearful, but he didn't. He's so tired from working long hours and he sees so much more than what we see but he is strong. I know he will look after us all.

WEDNESDAY, 2 MARCH

Poor Tessa, she read the Press this morning and the big headline is that her school, Avonside Girls' High, is so badly damaged they can't use it. They may have to share another school. I would so hate that. When I read the list of schools that might not be reopening, it made this all so much more real. It means we can't forget about this horrible earthquake because the damage is so much bigger than just broken buildings and broken pipes. There are all those people who have died and all the families who have had to leave the city, like Laura. Our lives have changed forever and I don't think they will ever be the same again. I think that is what scares me the most. That everything has changed forever and I don't feel safe any more.

Having days off school is normally fun but having a school that is too damaged to use is so strange. It's like what everyone says these days – that there is no normal any more, and all this destruction and devastation is our new normal. That's aftershocks too. People are also calling Christchurch 'munted'. And I think it is. My city is munted. Totally.

Dad had a day off today. He slept all morning and then he and Uncle Dave went back over to Pacific Park to dig up more of the horrible grey stuff. Tessa and I went too. More of Aunty Beth's neighbours have moved out. They still have no power or water. Lots of TV cameramen and reporters were there taking photos of the suburb as it is one of the worst hit. Uncle Dave said the house is still safe to live in if you don't mind all the cracks in the walls and floors. He says the council has said no one will ever be able to rebuild in this suburb as the risk of liquefaction is too high. Something to do with the type of soil under the houses being too sandy and swampy to build on safely. After we had dug up as much as we could, we headed home. The dust from the dried liquefaction was all up my nose and in my hair and skin. We must have breathed in a heap of it because we were all coughing for the rest of the day. Yuck! Sooo good for you . . . not!

When we got home, Dad flopped on the couch. I think he was trying to relax a bit but Jackson wouldn't leave him alone. I didn't watch the news tonight. Couldn't face it. Tessa didn't want to watch either so we hung out talking while Jackson played with his Lego.

Laura and I spent most of the night texting back and forth. She likes her new school and is going to see the choir teacher tomorrow to see if she can audition. I feel a bit jealous. She is safe and away from the aftershocks and all the nasty stuff we get bombarded with every day. I wish I could go to school in Timaru too.

THURSDAY, 3 MARCH

All over the radio and news is a warning not to flush toilets as the pipes are so bad and we need to conserve water. There is even a ditty everyone says. I hear it on the radio all the time: "If it's yellow, let it mellow. If it's brown, flush it down."

Jackson thinks it's funny and runs around the house saying it every time someone has to go to the toilet. "If it's yellow, let it mellow. If it's brown, flush it down. If it's yellow, let it mellow. If it's brown, flush it down." Then he giggles. At least he's having fun!

We still have to use the longdrop toilet outside, so we aren't flushing anything, but lots of people on the west side of the city still have flushing toilets.

It is tough trying to save water when Jackson wets the bed. He didn't use to, but since the earthquakes he's too scared to go outside at night. Dad gave him a bucket to use but I think he just goes by mistake. I know Mum is sick of wet bedding, but it isn't his fault. He's just anxious all the time.

Dusty came home today but she is thin and frail again. I made a bed for her next to mine, with her favourite blanket and a hot water bottle. Even Jackson has been checking up on her, patting her and just talking quietly. I was watching him from the hallway when he didn't know I was there. He kept telling her, "It'll be okay, Dusty. I know you're scared. I am too but it'll be okay. Good girl, Dusty. Go to sleep." He sounded so serious and grown up.

I guess we're all trying to make sense of things and just looking out for each other. That's one of the things people have been saying on the radio – that the earthquake has made people closer and more caring. People have been looking after each other and their neighbours. Seriously, though, why wouldn't we care? We have to care or it will all turn to a big mess. People are sharing houses and caravans and even living in garages and tents. Pretty much just fitting in where they can because so much has been damaged.

Aunty Beth wants to go back home but they still have no power or water so Dad said they have to stay here until they at least get water. It seems so strange that our side of the city has so much damage and the other side seems to be so safe. Although Dad says the other side of the city has lots of damage too but it is mostly inside the houses where you can't see it. On our side of town, what he calls the 'infrastructure' has been damaged. That's the roads, sewers, powerlines and stuff that keeps everything working and it's something everyone can see. But none of it is as bad as the centre of town where people have died.

FRIDAY, 4 MARCH

Today the paper reported that 161 people have died!

And the mayor says the number will go higher. I can't write any more today. I feel too sad. I just can't get my head around it. That's like all the Year 7 kids at my school gone – wiped out. I just can't believe it.

SATURDAY, 5 MARCH

Tessa and I went for a walk today. I just had to get out of the house. It's so crowded I felt as though I would burst or go mad or something if I didn't get out. Portaloos have popped up everywhere, like daffodils in springtime. Who would've ever thought that our streets would be lined with plastic toilets because we had no proper working sewerage system?

The water in our taps is still really dribbly and I so want a good long shower but we have to jump quickly in and out – and only every second day. Jackson loves it. He reckons it's cool not having to shower. With Aunty Beth and Uncle Dave still here, we have to take turns on odd days to help conserve water.

SUNDAY, 6 MARCH

This is what we now have in the boot of Dad's car – just in case:

Gumboots – for walking in liquefaction and potholes

Old garden spade – for digging liquefaction

Torch and batteries

Bottled water

Old jackets

Who in their right mind carries this much stuff in their car? Welcome to Christchurch!

TUESDAY, 8 MARCH

The council workers have been delivering chemical toilets to parts of Christchurch. They are horrible things. Once a week you have to empty all the smelly stuff into these great big, ugly, round containers that have been placed on footpaths on all the streets. Dad reckons if you let your toilet get too full, it would be so heavy that not everyone will be able to lift them high enough to empty them – and there will be splash back! Yuck! Poo everywhere!

How disgusting. I don't want to even think about it. I think our outside toilet looks pretty good compared to these plastic chemical ones. People are taking photos of their outside toilets. Some have got flowers and coffee tables next to them, making it all look a bit posh. Quite funny, really. I think there's a competition for the best outdoor dunny.

The mayor was in the paper and on TV showing people how to use the chemical toilet. Sometimes I can't help laughing at the whole thing. I mean, seriously, who would ever have thought we would need a lesson on how to use a toilet from the mayor? It makes me laugh.

WEDNESDAY, 9 MARCH

Aftershocks, useless water pressure, power on and off, crowded house and mess everywhere. I want to go away. I don't care where – just somewhere that isn't Christchurch.

Jackson and I went back to school today. Tessa still doesn't know what is happening but it looks like she is going to have to go all the way across town to Burnside High and share the school site. That is not going to be good!

The teachers at our school were great and wanted us to get straight back in to the school routine but everyone just kept talking about the earthquake and nothing much got done. We have to take our own bottled water as the water has been shut down. We have to use smelly portaloos and bring our own hand sanitiser. We're supposed to bring face masks from the chemist, too, for windy days when the dust blows everywhere. Most of us don't coz it makes you look geeky but there are a couple of kids who do. I think they get asthma, so guess the masks must help with that.

There are lots of kids still not back. Some have gone away for a few weeks and others have moved out of Christchurch altogether, because they can't live in their homes any more. I heard Zoe tell some of the girls that Bettina has gone to Hamilton to live – her house split right through the middle and her Mum doesn't want to live here. As much as I don't really like Zoe, I kind of feel sorry for her because she must be feeling like I do without Laura.

SATURDAY, 12 MARCH

Everyone is talking about a man called Ken Ring. They reckon he can predict earthquakes. Big ones! And he has predicted a big one – maybe even bigger than 22nd February – for March 20th. Everyone is scared and talking about leaving Christchurch. Dad told Tessa and me that the guy is wrong and you can't predict earthquakes. I **think** I believe Dad. I **want** to believe Dad … but part of me is scared just in case it's true. I don't think there's anything left to fall down in Christchurch and I really don't think we can take any more sadness. We've had enough.

SUNDAY, 13 MARCH

Aunty Beth and Uncle Dave moved back to their house today. They have to collect water from the tankers down the road but Aunty Beth just wants to be home, no matter if they have power or not. It comes on but goes off pretty often. She says if the power is out while they are at work it won't matter but she hopes they have it on at night. It is getting darker earlier too so I hope the power stays on.

MONDAY, 14 MARCH

One of the things we talked about in class today was the Memorial Day this Friday. All the schools will be closed so we can go and pay our respects to all the people who died. I'm not sure if I really want to go as it could be too sad. When I came home from school today, Mum was really upset. I asked her what was wrong but she wouldn't tell me. Jackson told me he heard her arguing on the phone about our chimney and not having heat for winter and asking when someone was coming to fix the roof properly. It got worse after the February quake and we don't have any other heat other than the log burner and that is munted now. I can't believe I'm now worrying about keeping warm in winter. Life sure has changed. Me too.

FRIDAY, 17 MARCH
Memorial Day

We stayed home from school today. Even Dad got the day off and we went in to Hagley Park for the memorial service. We had to park miles away as the central city is in the Red Zone and cordoned off with only soldiers, emergency workers and specialist people allowed in. The streets that are open are mostly down to one lane because of damage to the road. People were walking from everywhere. It was kind of eerie because no one talked much. There were just lots of people, all walking quietly.

The service was to remember all those who lost their lives in the quake, and all the people who are hurt and still missing. There were thousands of people there. It was amazing! I've never seen so many people in one place in Christchurch. Prince William came all the way from London. Yeah! The real live Prince William of England!! I can't believe how tall he is. Our Prime Minister was there, and also the Prime Minister of Australia, Julia Gillard.

We watched a video on the big screen, which showed the devastation in the city. It was so quiet and still on the video. Like a ghost town, all sad and abandoned. Food still sat on tables in the restaurants. I had been to so many of those places and now they are all destroyed or so damaged that they will have to be demolished. There was even a photo of the bookshop we go to and the shattered glass from all the windows was strewn all over the road. Everywhere was deadly silent. Really awful.

Many people spoke to us about how sad they felt but how we all need to stay strong for each other and that we will rebuild Christchurch and it will be better and stronger because of the earthquake. I don't think I'm convinced about rebuilding. I think it will be the most impossible job and with so much damage I think it will take forever to fix.

We had two minutes of silence at 12.51 and I have never seen so many people crying all at the same time. So many tears. Mostly there was silence as tears trickled down their faces. It was so awful but I also felt proud to be there. And when all the rescue workers came out, everyone stood up and clapped and cried. Then, when we all sang the national anthem, it was the strangest feeling because I felt sad and proud all at the same time. Tessa looked at me and I could tell she thought the same. I know she can be a pain but right there, at that moment, I was glad she was my sister.

I wish Laura could've been here though. Today I miss her so much. I know she was doing the 2-minute silence at her school, just like nearly the whole country.

It took ages to get home again and, when we did, I went straight to my room. I wanted to be alone to write my diary. I'm hiding it now in a different place every night. I don't want Mum or Dad to read it and see how scared I really am with all the aftershocks. I know they have enough to worry about and we all try to help Jackson and pretend things are going to be fine. If he feels better, he might stop wetting the bed. They don't need to know how afraid I am to go to bed at night, or how I keep my shoes right by my bed. If they knew I kept a bag under my bed with my favourite books, photos and things ready to just grab it and run, they might realise I am so terrified some nights that I stay awake, listening to every sound, waiting for the ground to move under my feet. I can't let them know because if I do, I might start crying and never stop.

SATURDAY, 18 MARCH

Aunty Beth and Uncle Dave have gone down to Invercargill to visit Gran. Aunty Beth says she isn't going to be here when the earthquake Ken Ring is predicting happens. Mum got so cross she swore at her!

"You can't predict earthquakes, Beth! It's scare-mongering and you're being silly," Mum shouted.

"Fine! You stay! But I'm out of here. My home is ruined and I'm not hanging around this weekend to see any more damage happen," Aunty Beth yelled back, and then they left.

I don't think I've ever heard them argue this bad before. I hope they don't stay mad at each other for long.

SUNDAY, 20 MARCH

It's 9.30 at night and so far, no big quake. That guy is wrong.

MONDAY, 21 MARCH

There were a lot of kids away from school today. I guess they've left town, like Aunty Beth, but we're having aftershocks every day anyway, so it doesn't make a lot of sense. It's the new normal!

I hate the new normal.

TUESDAY, 22 MARCH

Choir started up again today, which is okay, but I so miss Laura. Zoe was there and she looked a bit lost without Bettina but she pretended she was happy. Miss Broker, the choir teacher, asked us all to start thinking of some songs for a production. Not just random songs but songs with a theme for a special concert next term. Someone asked her what the theme was going to be and Miss Broker said it was just about making everyone smile again.

"I want everyone to brainstorm together and come up with some great ideas by next week. I know it isn't easy but we need to focus and carry on." she said and then let us go for the rest of lunchtime.

Zoe and some of the girls went in to a group and started talking. One of the girls asked me to join in too, but Zoe glared at me like I'd be dead meat if I did. I started to walk away and then thought of what Laura would have done. Laura would have joined in just to spite Zoe. So I turned back and smiled a big smile and joined in. I could feel Zoe's eyes burning in my back but I didn't care. Actually, the other girls are pretty cool and we talked all the rest of lunchtime. We didn't come up with any definite ideas but at least we tried. And it was nice to be talking about something other than the earthquakes.

WEDNESDAY, 23 MARCH

Laura rang tonight. It was so good to hear her voice. Tessa has been a miserable cow these last few days and won't even talk to me so hearing from Laura was awesome. Her Mum and Dad are hiring a trailer and coming up on Saturday to get some more things out of their house. I guess this really does means they are moving to Timaru for good.

Laura's going to spend the day at my house while her parents do stuff. It won't be for long but at least we can have lunch together and hang out. I can't wait. It feels like ages since we saw each other.

Mum came into my room tonight and sat on the bed. Next thing, she starts brushing my hair. She hasn't done that in years. We just talked. It felt good. Then we got the giggles because she brushed it so much my hair got full of electricity and was crackling and standing up on end.

SATURDAY, 26 MARCH
Laura's visit

I can't believe how much we talked. Non-stop. She told me all about her new school and her new friends and the house she is living in now.

"But you know what the best thing is?" she said. She didn't need to say it. I knew straight away what she was going to say. "No aftershocks. No rumbling. No shaking. And no being scared."

Right there and then I was so jealous of Laura I had to turn away so she couldn't see my face. But then she made me laugh when she did her impression of her new teacher. We had fish and chips for lunch and talked heaps more.

When her parents came to collect her, I knew straight away that her Mum had been crying. Laura's Dad said the house is a mess. It's even worse now than when they left – almost completely off its piles. All I know about piles is that they're to do with the foundations and it's not good if they are damaged. The roof is broken and leaks, and there's no power, water or sewerage. Where the liquefaction came up inside the house, there are now weeds. They showed us some photos and it looks awful. It looks even worse than Aunty Beth's house. Aunty Beth can still live in her house, even though it will be demolished eventually, but no one can live in Laura's house. It is barely standing up.

Laura looked really sad, but when she was leaving, her Mum said that they would bring her back to stay during the holidays or I could go down to Timaru.

"Can I?" I asked. "Oh, please!"

Laura jumped in then too and we both pleaded, "Please, please, please!"

"Just how are we supposed to say no to you girls?" Dad laughed.

Woohoo! Roll on holidays.

MONDAY, 28 MARCH

Tessa is in such a bad mood ALL the time. Her school is not going to reopen because of the damage, and from next week she will be going to Burnside High, way across the other side of town, where they will be sharing the site. The Burnside kids will start their school day earlier and finish at lunchtime, then the Avonside girls will start at lunchtime and go until about 5 o'clock. She'll need to take two buses to get to school and two to get home, by which time it will be about 6.30 p.m., and it is definitely getting darker at night now. Tessa is not going to like this one little bit. I don't blame her. I would hate to travel that far for school.

At least she'll get to sleep in longer in the mornings. When I told her that she just slammed the door on me, and yelled: "Yeah? Well, I've lost my job because I can't babysit the neighbours' kids after school any more. You know nothing! So just go away and leave me alone."

I should've felt sorry for her (and I do, really) but she just made me mad yelling like that. So now I've gone to bed in a bad mood. Good one, Tessa.

WEDNESDAY, 30 MARCH

At choir today, the teacher asked Zoe and I to sing together. We looked at each other and I know Zoe was going to argue with the teacher about it, but I just nudged her and said "Don't. We can do this." I hope like heck I can, because the last person in the world I want to sing with is that bully Zoe, but I also didn't want the teacher to give the chance to anyone else.

I really want to sing again. I feel so much better when I'm singing – I can kind of block out everything else that is happening around me. I can almost forget about the aftershocks and the fights with Tessa. I can almost forget about the noises in the middle of the night when Jackson has a nightmare and wakes up screaming. *Almost* forget ... but not really. Who am I kidding? Everywhere you look it's broken roads, broken buildings, broken city. Nothing is the same. But singing helps, so that's why I nudged Zoe.

I think she realised it too, and chose not to argue after that. We sang the song, which was pretty rough. Actually it was an epic fail but it was a new song and we hadn't done a duet together before. The teacher gave us a copy of the song each to take away and practise.

SATURDAY, 2 APRIL

I went out shopping with Mum today. Just the two of us, which was nice. We went to Tower Junction to look for a birthday present for Tessa. We got her a bright blue 3/4-sleeve top and jeans and a scarf to match.

There was a book lying open at the entrance of the bookshop, for people to sign their pledge to stay in Christchurch. Mum signed it straight away and then gave me the pen. I stared at her because she knows I hate it here now, but when I saw the look on her face I knew right then I had to sign it too. I also knew that I meant it, too, and that I do want to stay – and to do that I have to stop thinking about the earthquakes and start thinking about other things or I would just go crazy. So I signed it proudly under Mum's name.

At the counter they were selling black and red wrist bands – rubbery bands called Bands of Hope and the money goes to earthquake charities. Mum smiled and bought one for each of us. So shopping with Mum was good, and I came home feeling so much better and more positive than I have in ages. When we got home, we gave out the Bands of Hope. Even Dad wore a black one. It felt good to be part of something hopeful. Maybe, we will all get through this. Good days and bad days – but today was a good one.

SUNDAY, 3 APRIL

I got a text from Zoe this afternoon. I know I didn't give her my number so it's kind of freaky that she has it. She asked me to meet her at interval tomorrow by the art room. She wants to talk about our singing together. I couldn't tell by her text if she was happy about singing together or not. What if it's a set-up? What if she wants to beat me up? It wouldn't surprise me one little bit. I don't trust her.

I talked to Tessa about it but she just said not to be such a wimp and to give Zoe a chance. Then she almost yelled at me to "grow up". What did I do to deserve that? All I did was ask her advice. Honestly, I am so sick of her being grumpy. I know school is hard for her but ... argh!!! I sent a text to Laura to see what she thought, and she took ages to reply. I guess she has new friends now. All she said was just to be careful. I went to bed feeling very sorry for myself and dreading tomorrow morning and my meeting with Zoe.

MONDAY, 4 APRIL

I couldn't focus at all through Maths and got growled at for looking out the window. I caught Zoe grinning when the teacher told me off and that just made me feel even more nervous. When the bell finally went, Zoe followed me out of the classroom – and so did her friends. I was beginning to regret this and thought about running, but I knew Tessa and Laura would give me a hard time if they knew. So I went.

"You know, Maddy, you can sing. We all know that," Zoe said and the other girls nodded. Wow! I wasn't expecting that.

"But you know what your problem is? Focus!"

"Focus?" I asked.

"Yeah. You gotta learn to focus and be confident and not be scared to sing out strong and loud."

I must've been staring at her because she told me to close my mouth.

"Bettina is a better singer, but she isn't here and neither is Laura, so if you practise and stop being a wimp, you and I could do really well. We just need to practise together."

Again, I wasn't expecting that. I didn't know what to say. I mean, what do you say to someone who has bullied you for ages and then suddenly wants to start singing with you? So I just said, "Sure."

So that's what we're going to do. Every lunchtime Zoe and I are going to run through our song a couple of times until we get it right. I couldn't wait to text Laura and this time she answered straight away.

Weird but cool. U & Zoe, who wd've thought?

This could turn out okay.

Maybe …

TUESDAY, 5 APRIL

Zoe and I met at lunchtime today in the music room. I was nervous when we sang, but I was also determined that she wouldn't get a chance to have a go at me. And you know what? It was actually fun. Well, just a little bit of fun.

The music teacher said we could have the room for the first 15 minutes each lunchtime when everyone is supposed to be sitting and eating their lunch. If it means we have a chance to practise without anyone else watching, then I'm up for it.

WEDNESDAY, 6 APRIL

I didn't want to watch TV tonight so was on my bed reading when I heard Tessa in her room ... crying. I stuck my head in the door and she turned away.

"Go away," she snapped at me.

"No," I said, "not until you tell me what's wrong."

Then she looked at me, and her eyes filled up, and I felt so sorry for her. I sat down on the bed and she just started talking. I mean really talking, and I kind of felt like I was the big sister for a while.

"I hate going to school now. Everyone is nice at Burnside, but it isn't my school. I have to catch the bus and it's noisy and crowded and then we don't finish until 5.30. I get home so late ... and I just miss my old school ... and the trees by the river ... and it's just so unfair. I miss walking to school with Rosie. Everything sucks."

"Yeah, but it's the holidays soon ... and it's your birthday next week," I said.

"I don't need holidays. We've missed out on so much schoolwork, I'll never catch up. How can we fit everything in when our classes are now so short?" she said. "The teachers are trying to cram everything in and none of us can keep up." She looked so miserable I didn't know what to say so I just gave her a hug.

Then she told me to get out as she had heaps of homework to do but mumbled a quiet thanks as I went out the door.

I'm glad I can still walk to my school every day, and even though we don't have a school hall or swimming pool any more, at least we're able to still *go* to school.

MONDAY, 11 APRIL

Tessa's fifteenth birthday. Jackson and I wished her happy birthday before we left for school. We had a really late dinner last night, partly because Tessa didn't get home until ten to seven and also because Mum had a late haircut to do for someone. Dinner was Tessa's choice and she chose Chinese. It took Dad ages to get it as the takeaway place we usually go to was demolished after the earthquake so he had to go to one much further away. After dinner, Mum brought out a birthday cake and Jackson gave Tessa the present Mum and I had bought. I'm glad she liked the clothes. Aunty Beth and Uncle Dave turned up in time to share the cake. Aunty Beth gave her a Westfield Mall voucher and that certainly made Tessa smile. I gave her a copy of the Road Code as an extra present coz now she's old enough to learn to drive.

Went to bed feeling full. Too much cake!

TUESDAY, 12 APRIL

Zoe said if I wanted to practise during the holidays I could call her. Wow! Maybe I will if I don't have anything else to do. There isn't much to do these days. Mum won't let us go to the movies any more in case we have a big quake. Anyway, there are hardly any cinemas open now. Maybe we can have days just watching DVDs.

 # THURSDAY, 14 APRIL

I got an email from Laura today. She wants me to go down to Timaru for a few days in the holidays. Mum says she can drive me down in the middle weekend of the holidays. I can't wait! It will be so good to get together again. I'm going down on the Sunday and Laura's Mum and Dad will bring Laura and me back on the Thursday. They'll stay here a couple of days to do some shopping and check on their house.

 # SATURDAY, 16 APRIL

Holidays . . . and we start off by having a big 5.3 aftershock right on dinnertime. Even though they are still incredibly scary, we try to guess what magnitude the shakes are. Jackson has no idea and just calls out any number. It's really funny – "A hundred!" he'll shout. Totally random! Tessa was the closest this time – she said it would be at least a 5.1. At school we have competitions for who guesses the closest and our names go on the board if we get it right. When we get five correct or the closest we get a chocolate bar. It makes it a bit of fun and a easier to deal with if we focus on what we reckon the magnitude is.

WEDNESDAY, 20 APRIL

Nothing to write about really. We haven't been anywhere as Mum is busy doing haircuts. So we're just staying home and mucking around. I thought about ringing Zoe but chickened out.

THURSDAY, 21 APRIL

Today some men came to try and fix the roof. The tarpaulin has saved the ceilings from water damage but the fallen bricks from the chimney munted it. They've put up new roof tiles so there's no hole any more. They had to get a concrete cutter up in the roof space to remove the last of the chimney. What a noise! And so much dust!! It went everywhere.

Dusty took off down the back of the woodshed to get away from it all. The men said that EQC will arrange for a new ceiling in the lounge sometime but that it's okay for now. The tiles will keep the place watertight in the meantime. They're only doing emergency jobs at the moment, to make sure people have heat for winter.

Then some guys came and put in a heat pump. Mum's complaining about the cost of the power for the heat pump and Dad's complaining because Mum's complaining. I think I'd rather be at school. I spent ages vacuuming the lounge after the workmen left. Mum reckons if I do a few more jobs then she will give me some money for my holiday next week. So I've been dusting and wiping – or trying to wipe – the dust away. It just keeps coming back. There is so much of it from inside the roof.

 ## SUNDAY, 24 APRIL

Mum drove me down to Timaru today. Jackson came for the drive and he kept asking to stay with Laura and me. Before Mum left to return to Christchurch she handed me fifty bucks! "Spend it wisely," she said. I gave her a kiss and a hug. I'm so happy right now. I'm with Laura, I'm away from Christchurch, and I have money to spend. What more could I want?

MONDAY, 25 APRIL
Anzac Day

If I was in Christchurch I would probably have gone to the Anzac Day parade with Mum and Dad, although this year it isn't in Cathedral Square because that's still cordoned off. I think Dad said it was going to be in Hagley Park. Laura's family didn't go to any parade here in Timaru. Instead Laura, her Mum and I went to Caroline Bay. We walked around picking up shells and then we went and played mini golf in the afternoon. Laura beat me but that's okay. It is just so good to be doing things together. Later we did each other's hair and then painted our fingernails. Laura's Mum let us have her nail polish and we added glitter too so our nails look cool!

TUESDAY, 26 APRIL

Laura and I were dropped in town to do some shopping. We bought some silly stuff from a $2 shop because on Friday, when she stays with me, we are going to have our own Royal Party for the Royal Wedding. I bought some long-sleeved gloves and a plastic, blingy tiara. Her Mum picked us up after lunch and we went for a walk to Laura's school.

It is so cool. No cracked paths or gigantic piles of soil, and no portaloos around the place. I'd love to go to school here. Maybe I should run away and not go back to Christchurch. It won't ever happen, but it would be nice. I think. Sort of! I don't know really. I love Christchurch and it will be good to be part of rebuilding the city, but being here in Timaru makes me realise how unsafe I feel in Christchurch. I'm always waiting for something to happen, for something to go wrong.

Enough, Maddy, stop complaining! Now I'm talking to myself. LOL

THURSDAY, 28 APRIL

Laura's Mum and Dad drove us back home to Christchurch. Two hours and we sang almost all the way. Even her parents joined in. We must've looked like something out of an American TV show but it was fun. When we saw roadworks and potholes and signs and road cones everywhere, we knew we were getting closer to home. There was one sign on the footpath not far from our street.

Please slow down
Kids scared
Our houses are shaking

Yes, that told me I was back in Christchurch. Back to the shaking, chaos and craziness of my home town ... and all I wanted to do was turn around and go back to Timaru.

113

FRIDAY, 29 APRIL
The Royal Wedding

We spent most of today baking all sorts of things to tie in with our own Royal Wedding party. Laura and I made queen cakes and Mum made a pavlova. Tessa and her friend Rosie made cucumber sandwiches and club sandwiches. We even got some sparkling apple juice so we could have a drink to celebrate Prince William and Kate Middleton's wedding. Dad said we were all mad but we just laughed and told him there were lots of parties going on in New Zealand for the wedding. Aunty Beth and Uncle Dave came over after dinner and so did Laura's Mum and Dad. The men all went to the pub. Dad said they would come back when all the kerfuffle was over.

Before the wedding started on TV we put on our pyjamas and our tiaras, gloves and all our jewellery. I also wore Mum's old pearl necklace so I could look semi-posh. We looked ridiculous but that just made it even funnier.

The wedding was amazing. It was a bit long and boring in bits but Kate looked so beautiful. Her wedding dress was awesome and she really did look like a princess. She is so pretty and Prince William looked handsome in his uniform. When Kate's sister Pippa came out, she wore an amazing dress too. Tessa said she wished she had one like that. Mum said she'd have to take out another mortgage to pay for it. But you should've seen Princess

Beatrice's hat! Talk about weird – a real bizarre sort of sculptured funny brownish bow, way up high. Imagine if you were sitting behind it! I bet it was heavy and gave her a headache wearing it.

For a wedding present Prince William and Kate were given the titles Duke and Duchess of Cambridge.

We pigged out on so much food and sparkling apple juice, I thought I would pop. The men arrived home just before the end of the wedding. Dad grabbed my tiara and put it on his head. Then he put on this silly posh voice and said, "Oh yes, William . . . my dear, dear Willie, I *will* marry you. I do, I do, I definitely do." We all cracked up.

SATURDAY, 30 APRIL

Laura and her parents left just before lunch. They were going to check on what's left of their house and then do some shopping before going back to Timaru. We hugged goodbye but it wasn't long before she texted me:

At house. OMG It is awful. Not much left.

I texted back:

Oh no! So sorry. Hugs!

Everything about this earthquake is so random. Some houses stayed up and yet some houses next to each other fell down. It is just too weird and unfair.

SUNDAY, 1 MAY

At midnight the Mayor declared the state of emergency was over, but we had a couple of big shakes yesterday so I can't believe it will ever really be over.

There are still so many people living in garages with outdoor toilets or those chemical ones. Aunty Beth still has days without power, and water that just dribbles out of the tap. Whenever she comes over she has a shower. The other day, she had the longest shower ever, but reckons she'll never get rid of the smell.

Workmen have to come around the streets to pump out the sewer pipes as the water damage means they don't flow the way they used to, and sometimes there is splashback. Gross! In some places you have to keep a brick on top of your toilet lid to hold it down. Aunty Beth had forgotten to put the brick on and when the men pumped out the pipes in her street, heaps of poo and gunk came up through the pipes into her toilet! Mega-gross!!!

She took photos for insurance in case she needed them. It was soooo disgusting! The mess was up the walls and over the floor. It's not even your own poo – it could be anyone's. I felt like throwing up when she showed us the photos. It took her ages to clean it up and disinfect everything and to be honest she did actually smell a bit afterwards. We really are so lucky at our place. For lots of reasons.

It's cold most days now but at least we have some heat. I miss the log burner though. That gave really good heat. It's funny, but seeing the flames in the log burner used to make me feel warmer. Must be one of those psychological things. The heat pump is okay but sometimes the power goes off, although not usually for too long, thank goodness. It's a pain when we're trying to cook dinner or watch TV, but some houses still have no power at all so I won't complain.

At night we have hot water bottles to keep our toes warm in bed, although Dusty tries to sleep on top of my feet when she can. She snuggles in tight and when it gets really cold she climbs under the blankets with me. Then she starts purring, but I can listen to that all night. It is kind of comforting and she is so soft and warm.

MONDAY, 2 MAY

Second term started today and Zoe cornered me at morning tea and said we urgently had to practise our singing. I said it was only the first day back, and why was she so desperate. She gave me one of her old bullying Zoe glares so I tried walking away, but she grabbed my elbow. I waited for her to do something awful, but instead she said, very quietly so I almost didn't hear, that we could end up on TV on the Rise-Up Telethon.

"Do you know anything about it?" she asked.

"Of course," I said. "It's to raise money for the earthquake fund'.

She said if we practised we could go to the telethon and we might end up on TV. I told her I would think about it and talk to her at lunchtime. She shrugged and walked off.

Well, I couldn't think of anything else after that! Singing. TV. Zoe. Singing. TV. Zoe. By lunchtime I'd decided I'd give it a go. Who knows, it might be fun. So we ran through our songs a few times, then agreed to meet every lunchtime for the rest of the week. Miss Broker thought it was a good idea too. She said with the production later this term, we might end up being the opening act.

TUESDAY, 10 MAY

Zoe and I sing every day and it's tolerable – sort of – but as soon as we're done, we go and hang out with our own friends. We aren't ever going to be besties but at least I'm not afraid of her any more. That's a good feeling. I told Tessa that, but she wasn't really interested. I guess things are still hard for her but I can't make it better.

We have to wait for her to get home from school before we have dinner, which means it's always so late and Jackson is tired by then. And she doesn't laugh much any more. When she does smile, it's like a crumpled-up fake one. I miss my sister even though she's right in front of me. It's like she's disappeared and been replaced by a zombie. I know there is no easy answer to all this. There is no quick fix and we all have to pick ourselves up and carry on, but some days are just a lot harder than others.

THURSDAY, 12 MAY

There was an article on the front page of the Press today all about the CTV building. 116 people died when it collapsed. I can't believe so many people died in just one building. Many of them were students from Japan who came to Christchurch to learn English. It is just so, so unfair. One of Mum's friends was standing in Latimer Square when it collapsed. She still has nightmares about it. Seeing all the CTV rubble on TV is bad enough, but to have seen it actually happen must've been horrific.

SATURDAY, 14 MAY

I wrote a poem today. Normally I don't like writing poetry but I've been thinking about all the buildings that are going to be pulled down and I just had to write something.

DEMOLITION DAY

ONCE STOIC AND PROUD
THE OLD BUILDING NOW LISTS SIDEWAYS.
"DEMOLISH" THEY SAY
"TOO DAMAGED
TOO DANGEROUS".

IN COME THE DIGGERS
IN COME THE DOZERS
DOWN
DOWN
DOWN.
ONCE BRICKS AND MORTAR
NOW JUST
DIRT AND DUST.

SUNDAY, 15 MAY
Share an Idea Expo

Today the whole family went to the Share an Idea Expo. It was for everyone in the city to write down their ideas about how we want Christchurch to look in the future. We watched the video that we'd seen at the Memorial Day and it was still awful and eerie and just so surreal.

There were computers set up so people could enter their ideas but there were lots of queues so we wrote our ideas down on post-it notes and stuck them on great big partitions. I walked around reading what other people wrote. There were heaps of notes from people wanting more cycleways and more green areas and parks. Some people want trams going from town to the university. Others want places to walk their dogs. Some people want to keep the heritage buildings, and others suggest bulldozing the lot and make everything modern.

It's going to be impossible to make everyone happy. I don't think the council can manage that. Like Mum always says: You can please some of the people some of the time, and some of the people all of the time, or all of the people some of the time – but never all of the people all of the time!! We've been talking over different ideas for our city at school, too, The teachers say we are the ones who are going to be living and working in the new Christchurch, so we need to put our ideas forward or we won't ever get heard.

My ideas are:

* Lots of green spaces.
* More places for young people to hang out.
* NO high-rise buildings. (Too scared to go in them!)
* Places should be open and safe.
* Need places for drama schools with new stages.

Jackson asked me to write down his idea too – a Lego park. I wrote it down, even though it's not even remotely possible and won't ever get considered. But I couldn't help smiling as it's not a bad idea for a 6-year-old.

Dad drove us out to Sumner after the expo. It's the first time I've been there since before the earthquakes last year. There are shipping containers lined all along the road protecting the roads from rock fall. When we got into Sumner I could see the rocks that had fallen. They were a burnt orange colour and some of them were ginormous. You had to wonder how rescuers could find anyone under the rubble – someone had died under those rocks. Even now I still get shocked by what I see and the stories I hear.

We called in to see Aunty Beth on the drive back. I couldn't believe how bad the roads had become since the last time I was here – they look like they've been bombed! Dad complained the roads were ruining his tyres.

I thought that was hilarious. "Aren't *you* supposed to fix the roads, Dad?"

He laughed too and so did Tessa.

SUNDAY, 22 MAY
Rise-Up Telethon

Mum dropped Tessa, Rosie, Jackson and me at the telethon. I met up with Zoe and her friends by the entrance. I was stuck with Jackson, which didn't please Zoe, but Tessa promised to come back and get him if we got to sing. There were lots of other people singing too and we'll all get a chance to perform, but not all of it will be shown on TV. There were heaps people there and I started to get nervous but Zoe reminded me to focus. They've brought some famous people down here to help raise money for the Christchurch Earthquake Fund but when I saw Rachel Hunter – supermodel!! – I was a bit gobsmacked. She has this amazing hair, and looks really tall.

One of the workers pulled Zoe and me aside and said we could go on next and just sing. He told us reporters might be talking over us but we were to just keep singing. It would be difficult because it was so noisy and I was having second thoughts when Tessa pulled me aside and said, "Take a deep breath, Maddy, I know you'll be awesome." It took me by surprise, after the way she's been behaving lately but I gave her a quick hug and thanked her although I was still just as nervous. Then she took Jackson's hand and moved to the area in front of the stage. Zoe and I were shunted on to the stage area and told to just start singing. So we did. And it felt good. Even with Zoe it felt awesome to be up there, singing in front of people. When we finished, Jackson was jumping up and down, all excited. Zoe gave me a high five and said "We did it!" and then left with her friends. It was a pretty awesome day. I spent most of the night texting Laura until Mum came in and told me off.

"That cell phone is not a toy, Maddy," she said.

"I know," I said – and texted Laura goodnight.

The telethon raised over $2.5 million, which is brilliant. It was an EXCELLENT day!

MONDAY, 23 MAY

Some of the kids at school came up and said they had seen Zoe and me on TV and thought we did a good job. Some wanted to know if we met Rachel Hunter and what was she like.

Miss Broker called a meeting for all of us in the choir. She gave us handouts of song words and told us that we will all be singing as a choir in the production, plus some of us will sing duets and we'll all be singing in the background when the dance team performs. The drama team will do a few skits too, and the orchestra will perform as well. Because it's going to be a bigger production than she first thought, it will now be in the middle of Term 3. All the songs and performances are going to have a theme running through them that ties them all together with a grand finale involving the choir and orchestra.

After listening to everyone's ideas over the last few weeks the principal has said it is going to be like a spring gala, starting with songs and dances from old musicals and ending up with more modern songs. Miss Broker asked if any of us had watched *Glee*. Almost all our hands went up.

"Well, we hope to have a big performance like they do on that show," she said. "Who is up for it?"

Every hand went up. Some cheered and others woohooed. It's going to be awesome! For the first time in ages I really feel like things are getting better. Miss Broker told Zoe and me she had seen us on the telethon and said we did a great job. She also told us that we would definitely be doing the opening song in the school production. My turn to woohoo!

WEDNESDAY, 25 MAY

It's been two whole weeks since Jackson last wet the bed. Hooray! Good on you, Jackson. He gets so embarrassed but it isn't his fault.

He must be feeling better too. Mum made him a sticker chart – if he goes two weeks straight without wetting the bed he can choose takeaways. So tonight Dad's going out to get pizza. Some pizza places don't deliver any more, or won't go to certain streets because the roads are too damaged. Aunty Beth says the postman hasn't really delivered mail to her street since the earthquakes so they get all their mail redirected to Uncle Dave's work. Seems the footpaths are too dangerous and bumpy for the bikes. "At least it stops the junk mail," she says.

SUNDAY, 29 MAY

Laura and I talked on the phone for ages today. It's her birthday tomorrow and she'll be 12. She had an early party today with her new friends. I wish I could've gone but it's a two-hour drive – too far just for a party, and Mum didn't have time to take me anyway. Laura and her dad made cupcakes for the party. If this stupid earthquake hadn't have happened, it would've been me making the cupcakes with her.

That got me thinking about singing and I guess if I really thought about things it would probably be Laura and Zoe singing the duet in the school production next term if she was still here. Part of me feels guilty that it's going to be me singing, because I know Laura is much better than me, but part of me is glad she isn't here as I would never have got the chance otherwise.

Tessa's still cranky and bad tempered. She wants to learn to drive but Dad says the roads are just too messy in the east where we live, and he says he hasn't got time to drive her over to Burnside or Hornby for a lesson when he only gets Sunday off and she gets home too late from school during the week. Wow, did she go off when Dad said that. Even I took off because she was so fired up.

MONDAY, 30 MAY

Tessa's still in a grump. I am **so** going to keep out of her way. All day. Or maybe all week even. Or maybe until she leaves home and gets married. Even Jackson is learning to avoid Tessa but then he wants to hang around me more. I can't win!

WEDNESDAY, 1 JUNE

School was awesome. We're going to be having a dance on the last day of term. Mr Thompson says we need to do something just for fun. It won't even be a fundraiser, just a good old dance "to brush away the cobwebs," he says. I can't wait.

I walked home from school today with Bella, a girl in my class. She's quite nice and it's better than walking home on my own. When we got to the dairy I bought a can of fizzy drink and a bag of lollies. She bought some stuff too and then we sat by the bus stop to eat, drink and talk.

Bella's in the orchestra and told me that she liked Zoe's and my singing. She told me she plays the violin because she can't sing a note in tune. That's funny – I sing but I can't play an instrument to save myself. I tried piano once but I just couldn't make my hands do different things at the same time. We talked about the dance. I think she likes Ben, a boy who sits in the back of the class. He gets into trouble a bit with the teachers for being 'disruptive' ... but he is funny. And his friend Alex is kind of cool. It was good having someone else to talk to.

I told Tessa about the dance but she wasn't interested. In fact she just moaned that while us mere intermediate kids were planning a dumb dance she would be stuck studying all day and all night trying to catch up on all the time she missed when her school was closed.

Why is everything **my** fault. Grrrrr!

THURSDAY, 2 JUNE

Today I got stuck in to Tessa and I told her I'd had enough of her being stroppy with me. It kind of went something like this.

ME: Talk to me.

HER: What do you know about anything? You're just a kid.

ME: I am **not** just a kid, and anyway I'm your sister, and I hate seeing you like this.

HER: You don't get it.

ME: Don't get what? I've been through the earthquakes too, you know.

HER: I know ... it's just that ... it's just ...

And then she started crying!

ME: [almost shouting] Just what?

HER: Just that I am so scared all the time. Scared of every sound ... every rumble of a truck or bus. I'm scared to sleep, I'm scared to be awake. I'm scared all the time –and I'm the oldest. I should be strong for you and Jackson.

I started crying then too and I don't know how long we cried for together. It seemed ages.

HER: It's all everyone talks about, and I hate going to the other school. I want my school. I want the broken things to be fixed again and everything to be back the way it was. And I feel guilty, get it? I feel guilty because we are all alive and others died. I am so confused and scared all the time. I hate it, hate it, hate it!"

And that was when I realised that I felt just the same and I knew that both of us had just been pretending to cope. Right then I knew we had to talk to each other more. Hugs weren't enough. I knew then that these earthquakes had changed me and my family forever and I hated it too.

Finally, I could let it all out as well, and we talked and cried for ages. I told her how scared I was too, and how bad I felt that some kids at school just didn't seem to be affected at all. Why couldn't I be like them? I think it's just part of living in a disaster zone and trying to live a normal life in a very un-normal city.

I am sooo glad we talked tonight.

 ## SATURDAY, 4 JUNE

You know, I think Christchurch has become a city of colours. Everywhere you look there are posters and signs up on walls and buildings telling us which ones are safe and which ones aren't. Heaps of 'Danger' signs are stuck up everywhere too.

Green signs / yellow signs / red signs. Safe / needs serious checking / and keep out – seriously dangerous! I know the colours are important but there are just so many red-stickered buildings, which means those buildings will probably be demolished. There won't be be much left in town when you look at all the red-stickered buildings.

There are heaps of people wearing fluoro orange or yellow high-visibility jackets. Dad wears an orange one when he goes to work. So many drivers are crazy when they drive and impatient because of all the road works, detours and delays, and I worry that Dad will get bowled by a car.

He says, "That's why I wear the vest, Maddy. It keeps me seen and safe."

Then there are the dreaded orange road cones on every street. Up the street, along the riverbank and down by the shops. There are road cones everywhere! Dad jokes he'd be rich if he got 50 cents for every damaged road cone he finds each morning.

Even the portaloos up and down the streets are different colours.

I've been thinking about the things I miss:

* all the cool stuff you could do at Science Alive
* going to the movies, especially Hoyts, and playing air hockey after the movie
* just walking on undamaged footpaths and not having to think about falling over

* The Children's Bookshop

* going to the museum and the art gallery

* walking through the Arts Centre

* buying walnut fudge from Fudge Cottage in the middle of the old buildings at the Arts Centre.

And, even though I haven't been for ages, probably years really, I suddenly want to go to the aquarium – but that's out too. There really isn't a heck of a lot left to do in Christchurch.

MONDAY, 6 JUNE
Queen's Birthday

It is Queen's Birthday weekend, so no school today It's not actually her real birthday, but for some reason it's a holiday for us. I spent ages reading in bed this morning coz it was warmer in bed than anywhere else in the house. Even with the new heat pump the house still has places where it is cold. The heat doesn't come into the bedrooms unless we open the doors and then there's no privacy and Jackson just wanders in and jumps on my bed.

The house has cracks and the windows are all draughty where they have buckled in the corners. I know they'll be fixed one day. Meantime, we put rolled-up towels along the windowsills, and Dad's put duct tape around most of them (to stop the cold air and wind getting in through the gaps). Mum says it could be years before repairs are made as there are too many houses that have been damaged. Thousands of people are still waiting to have their homes checked out by EQC and thousands aren't even allowed in their houses (like Laura) in case they fall down in another big shake. Winter just makes it worse, when I think about the people who still have to use outside toilets or have windows and walls all boarded up.

After I finally got up and dressed, Tessa and I went for a walk up to the video place and hired a couple of movies. When we got home Jackson stuck his nose up at our choice of DVD and went and played Lego in the kitchen with Dad, who had the day off. Mum sat with us and watched the movie too, so we popped a heap of popcorn and completely pigged out. It was a good day.

THURSDAY, 9 JUNE

Choir practice was soooo good. I can't believe it. Not only will Zoe and I open the production, singing with the orchestra, but the teacher asked if we would also sing a song from the movie *Grease*. I love that movie! I could watch it over and over again. She says we can decide which one we want to do, so Zoe and I plan to do that tomorrow at lunchtime.

FRIDAY, 10 JUNE

Couldn't agree on a song so will choose next week.

MONDAY, 13 JUNE

No. No. No. No. No. NO! Not again!

I don't believe it. Please tell me this is not happening again.

I don't want to be here. I want to leave and never come back. We **s**houldn't have to live like this. This is NOT normal.

Why? Why? WHY?

I don't understand why this keeps happening.

At lunchtime today we had a massive 5.0 aftershock. What is it with lunchtimes? We were all outside finishing our lunches and talking. I was with Zoe when it hit because we were still trying to decide which *Grease* song we could sing for the school production. Then this massive aftershock rumbled through the school grounds, knocking things down and terrifying us all. Even the trees were swaying under the pressure and kids all over school began screaming. We immediately dropped into our turtle positions for safety.

Once the shaking stopped we grabbed each other and ran to our safety lines on the tennis courts. I texted Tessa straight away and she said she was okay but it would probably be hours before she would get home. Mr Thompson said we were allowed to go home with our parents when they came to collect us or if we showed them we had a text from our parents telling us we could leave.

Mum texted me to get home quickly as she was heading to get Jackson. I knew that was fair and made sense but I still felt a bit disappointed that she wouldn't be able to come and walk home with me. I knew I could do it but it didn't stop me from being scared. It wasn't too far to walk but I didn't want to go alone. Luckily I saw Bella and we walked home together.

All the way home we could hear sirens everywhere and horns beeping. We saw cars blocking traffic and drivers just trying to get places. It is a bit like madness and panic but, in a strange way, the panic is almost polite – if that makes sense. This has happened so many times now that it almost feels normal and people just do what they have to do. When we got near the dairy, Bella went in one direction and I ran the rest of the way home in the other direction.

I was puffed out by the time I got there but so glad to be home. Mum had said I wasn't to go in the house until she and Jackson got there. She wanted to make sure the place was safe before anyone went in. At least the house was still standing. I tried texting Dad but he didn't reply, which made me worried. Mum and Jackson got home about 2.15 and Mum made me stay outside with Jackson while she checked inside the house to see if there was any more damage.

Jackson was whimpering again. Poor boy! If I'm scared then he must be even more scared. Actually I don't know anyone who wouldn't be scared living like this. While we were waiting for Mum we had an even bigger aftershock, if you can believe that. Jackson and I were sitting on the stump of the old cherry tree on the front lawn when it hit. We could see the ground surging towards us like it was heaving its guts, spewing out its insides trying to knock us off our feet. The ground was buckling, going up and down and up and down. Jackson and I screamed.

Even though we heard the roar first, it still just came out of nowhere. I grabbed him and pushed him down on to the ground without even really thinking about it, but all I could see was the power lines above us, which lead into the house, and they were swinging like crazy – like someone was tossing them and pulling them with invisible string backwards and forwards, backwards and forwards. I kept thinking that the force and speed was so strong that if they snapped we would die. We wouldn't be able to outrun snapped power lines.

They kept swinging above us and I was so terrified. I didn't know how I would save us both. So I just covered Jackson with my body and we froze where we were. I think I prayed. Yeah. I know I prayed. Loud and long. I kept thinking, *I don't want to die, I don't want to die.*

Mum came running out then and we stayed outside for ages talking with neighbours who had also all come out. I don't know where I feel safest, inside or outside. After a while we went inside and sat on the couch, dumbstruck that this could happen again.

Tessa and Dad came home together and found us still sitting on the couch. Dad guessed the buses probably wouldn't be running and, knowing Tessa was all the way on the other side of town, he just went to Burnside and collected her. It was really good to see them both when they got in.

You know, I've cried so much this year, I haven't got any more tears left. I just feel numb. I never dreamt in a million years that we would have a massive earthquake. And not just once – this is our fourth big one. Not counting the smaller tremors we have every week.

Doesn't Mother Nature know we have nothing left?

I WANT IT TO STOP!!!

It doesn't matter where you go in Christchurch there are reminders everywhere. Ruined houses sunk in the ground or split through the middle. Buckled and warped roads dotted with road cones lined up like soldiers, guarding the holes and traps. Corners where the shops have been demolished and rubble piled up.

I feel sad but I don't want to. Sometimes I feel guilty because Laura lost her home and had to move ... Aunty

Beth and Uncle Dave are going to lose their new home near the wetlands … Gran's gone to Invercargill and I know Mum misses her heaps. I feel guilty because we still have our house. Even with all the damage to the roof, and chimney and Mum's car and even all the broken things inside, we still have a home. It looks messy and a bit munted in places and it is cold but we can still live here and it is all I have ever known. I would hate to lose all this. I feel guilty because I am lucky.

I've been thinking about Gran all day today. She would hate it here. I hate it here. No one outside Christchurch understands. Not even Laura any more. She took ages to answer my texts then she said she had to go as she had things on after school. That made me cry. Jackson is a right pain too. He keeps shouting and following me around. Nothing seems fair any more.

Aunty Beth and Uncle Dave came over tonight. They've got no power or water AGAIN. They were yelling at each other too. She wants to pack up and leave Christchurch and he is so angry with the council he wants to stay and fight for every cent he can get from them. Their road and drive and lawn are covered in liquefaction again. Uncle Dave kept saying he was 'sick of digging the bloody stuff up'.

He even shouted at Mum and Dad, that "It's *inside* the house this time. The damn stuff is in the corners of the lounge where you can feel the cracks in the floor. The house will fall down around us by the time the council, insurance and bloomin' government make up their minds on how to fix things."

He scared me, he was so angry. I thought he was going to punch the walls in. Dad told him to calm down but that just made him madder. They went out to the garage for ages.

Tessa shut herself in her room and wouldn't come out. Listening to music on her iPod, I guess. I sat with Jackson on his bed for ages and read him some of his picture books. And the whole time the ground kept rolling and growling like some wild animal trapped in a cage, trying to get out.

TUESDAY, 14 JUNE

No school today. This is ridiculous. We have missed so much school this year, how on earth are we going to catch up?

We're back to boiling water again. Just in case! Just in case of what? I ask. Just in case we all catch horrible germs, diseases, stomach aches, and diarrhoea. Who knows? We might even catch the plague.

I slept in my clothes again with the torch at the ready. We all know what to do now, but it doesn't mean I will ever get used to ducking for cover, or living in fear. I spent the day picking up things that had fallen down. Even though I never put my books back in the bookcase these days and just pile them up in the wardrobe, they still fell down. Aunty Beth reckons she has nothing left in her house to break. They still have no power and I bet the food in the freezer will need to be thrown out again unless the power comes on soon. At least we have power.

I watched the news and the Cathedral in the middle of the Square has a lot more damage. That awesome big rose window has fallen in. I'm not sure why, but knowing that beautiful window has gone made me cry. It looks kind of derelict and sad like it had been abandoned years ago. If you could pick it up and put the cathedral in a forest somewhere it would look a bit haunted. It is just incredibly sad that all these historic buildings have been damaged. Our history is gone and it only took seconds for it to crumple and fall and change our city forever.

Dad had to drive through Opawa this morning to pick up one of his work mates and he said there was a group of shops that had been damaged in February's quake but had still been standing last week. When he saw them today, the whole lot had collapsed in a pile of broken rubble. The corner shop, with its big red brick wall, was the place where we bought all our bikes. He said it looked like a bomb had gone off. It is so random how the aftershocks can cause so much destruction in one place and hardly anything in another.

I got a surprise this afternoon when Zoe texted me to see if I was okay. Weird, but actually kind of nice. Her family and house are okay although there's a few more cracks in the walls, like us. I think she was just bored with everything. I haven't had any texts from Laura today. I guess everything in Timaru is normal and she's at school.

I told Tessa about Laura and she just gave me a hug. Then she said that people change, they grow apart, and that Laura probably has new friends now, just like I do. I guess you could count Bella and maybe even just a little bit Zoe (and I mean just a *tiny* bit), as my new friends. Tessa said it wasn't that Laura wasn't my friend any more, it was just that we are living different lives now and hers doesn't include earthquakes.

"Maybe, hearing about the aftershocks makes Laura feel guilty that she's not here any more, having to go through them like you do. Sometimes when you feel guilty you just try to avoid things."

I really don't get Tessa. Sometimes she is the best, most wonderful, sensible sister on the whole planet, and other times I wish she WAS on another planet, altogether.

It doesn't matter, I guess because I know that deep down Laura and I are still best friends and we always will be, no matter what Tessa was trying to say. It took ages to get to sleep tonight. Not just because of all the aftershocks rocking the house and keeping us awake, but because I still wasn't really sure about Laura and me being best friends any more – or about anything any more. Maybe Tessa is right.

WEDNESDAY, 15 JUNE

We drove over to Aunty Beth's this morning and there were so many more road cones and more roads closed off. They lost power again and we spent time digging up the horrible, grey, sludgy liquefaction. It's like living in a movie – the one where the same thing happens again and again. I think it is called Groundhog Day or something like that. Only this is real and not some movie we can turn off and forget about. Even Jackson got a bucket and tried digging up the gunk and piling it on the road. The council only gives you so many days to pile all the sludge on the road. Then they send trucks around to collect it all.

I thought about Laura and her family. How can they be expected to dig up liquefaction if they are living in Timaru? I wonder what will happen to all the liquefaction in the abandoned houses. Sometimes this whole horrible earthquake thing is too big to think about. Earthquakes, dead people, injured people, insurance, EQC and councils, and everything else just makes my brain hurt. I want it all to just go away or be back the way it used to be.

I tried singing around the house when we got home to stop me from going crazy but Mum told me to stop. Dad went to bed for a while when we got home as he is working nights at the moment. "The road repairs don't stop just because it's nighttime, Maddy," Mum said in her just-do-as-I-say voice. I do worry that someone might not see him at night and knock him over but he says there are so many road cones and his high-vis coat lets drivers know he is there. Also, they work in big groups and block off lanes so you can't help but see them.

When he works nights, Dad has to sleep during the day – which is easy when we are at school – but we ARE NOT AT SCHOOL. AGAIN!

I wrote all sorts of stuff in my diary last night when I was really angry. Looking back over it, nothing I wrote made any sense. I sounded like a madman so I crossed great big lines through the middle of it and started again.

Later I checked on the school website and it says we should be able to go back to school tomorrow as all the buildings will have been checked.

THURSDAY, 16 JUNE

School is open today. Hooray! At assembly on the courts Mr Thompson told us that if any of us weren't coping we could go and talk to him. None of us would ever admit we weren't coping so it was bit weird, but there is so much in the papers and on the radio about not coping that it's a bit scary thinking about it. Some kids at school don't really care at all. They are mostly the ones whose homes are fine and haven't lost anything.

Some kids cry easily. Dad reckons we don't really have a choice about what is happening and that we just need to get on with life and be grateful. Mum hovers somewhere in between agreeing with Dad and then giving us extra hugs with tears. I'm somewhere in between too. I think Tessa is as well – and Jackson? Well, he's only six and he is wetting the bed again so I guess he isn't coping all that well. It's just not fair. I thought the aftershocks were over and that life was going to get better. Perhaps it isn't. Maybe this is the way it will be forever in Christchurch.

Anyway, now kids at school are more concerned about the dance at the end of the month than the earthquakes. Mum said if I stopped arguing with Tessa she might buy me some new jeans and a top for the dance. Awesome! She's been getting lots more clients lately. Well, she was up until Monday's quake. Hopefully, next week people will start coming back. More people want to get their hair cut somewhere local these days as the roads are too unreliable – one day they'll be open, the next they're closed off.

Lots of old ladies come in wanting a perm. Mum usually puts on a DVD for them and gives them cups of tea. There are a couple of regular ones she goes and picks up from the rest home around the corner. There are two old ladies, in particular, who are Mum's favourites. I like them too. They are so funny. They are both widows who have lived in the rest home for years. I think one is 89 and the other is 91.They laugh a lot and gossip about the other people in the rest home. Sometimes they even sing old songs from the forties and fifties and Mum joins in too. She's always in a good mood after they have been.

FRIDAY, 17 JUNE

I finally caught up with Zoe at interval today and we made a choice about what *Grease* song we want to sing. We thought we might do the Sandra Dee song and dress up the same and make it fun and a bit funky – a bit over the top. I've learnt a lot of things this year, and one thing in particular is that we need to laugh more and that includes laughing at ourselves.

We checked with Miss Broker and she said we could do it as long as we still remember all the other songs, and she told us we weren't allowed to slacken off but had to stay focused. We both thought it was a bit much asking anyone in Christchurch to stay focused these days, but it's all good.

I hunted through Mum's old DVDs looking for her copy of *Grease*. FINALLY found it hidden in the back of the garage behind some of the boxes of broken stuff from the earthquakes. I don't know how long we have to keep all the broken TVs and smashed crockery in the garage but Dad says the EQC and insurance company said we have to keep it all as proof. Who needs proof that we had an earthquake? How stupid is that? Almost everyone in Christchurch has a garage full of broken stuff. And those with broken garages keep their stuff in crates or with family or friends. Lots of people just leave things like furniture on the streets with big signs saying 'Free!' You're not supposed to do it but heaps of people do, and anyway, it doesn't take long before the stuff disappears.

SUNDAY, 19 JUNE

I've decided I no longer like weekends. Not quite true, I guess. I still do like them, it's just that there isn't much to do here any more. Most of the movie theatres are still closed and damaged so we can't do that. And anyway I don't want to sit in the dark with loud noises, not knowing if they are coming from the movie or if it might be an aftershock starting up. Mum wouldn't let us go anyway. I don't like going into malls to shop any more, which I used to love doing before the quakes. Now I have to know exactly where the exits are and how quickly I can get out of a place before I go in. It is such a strange feeling. If we do go anywhere, we all check out the buildings and look for cracks. It's sort of funny because you walk in somewhere new or somewhere you haven't been for ages and suddenly you see everyone's eyes roving around the buildings, looking in corners and looking for escape routes. I don't know if it is funny or scary but it is all very surreal and normal now.

Even though Bella and I are kind of friends – and maybe even Zoe – we don't hang out on weekends. I end up stuck at home with Jackson following me around wanting to play, and Tessa being a bad-tempered pain in the neck. Mum and Dad go on about how we have to let her study quietly because she's lost so much school time.

I did spend time texting with Laura tonight. She says her dad has to come back to Christchurch for work. He's going to stay in a motel to start with, but if he can find a house to rent, they might move back. With so many houses damaged, rentals are hard to get, and they might end up on the other side of town, which means we won't go to the same school. But that would be okay. We could still talk on the phone and see each other at weekends. I told her I'd cross all my fingers and toes for luck. (Ever tried texting with your fingers crossed? Not so easy.)

I reckon, though, that she won't be too sad if she doesn't get to move back up to Christchurch. She has lots of new friends in Timaru. She says she's a bit like a celebrity because everyone wants to know what it was like living through the earthquakes, and everyone is really nice to her. There are some other kids at her school who also moved down there after the February earthquake and people are nice to them, too. I so badly want her dad to find a place to live so she comes back. I miss spending time with her, making cupcakes, being silly and singing. Singing is good with Zoe ... but singing with Laura is better. I started to hum that song from *Grease* about how we go together like rama-rama-something-or-other ... and that's how it is with Laura. We go together well. I really hope she comes back. That would be the best thing ever.

MONDAY, 20 JUNE

When I got home from school, Mum was waiting for me. Like, as soon as I got in the house, she took my hand and walked me into the lounge. I knew it had to be something bad.

She said she had sad news. Mrs Williams from next door had died on the weekend. We haven't seen her since she moved away to live with her son. Apparently, the earthquakes were just too much for her. She was always scared and she just got very tired and weak and stopped eating. I felt so sad when Mum told me that. She said a lot of old people who had moved out of Christchurch after February's earthquake had died, not long after moving into other rest homes. Many of them missed their families and it was just too hard for them.

"What about Gran?" I asked.

"Gran's tough, Maddy. She'll be just fine," Mum said.

Poor Mrs Williams. It's sad that her house has been empty all these months and now she won't ever come back.

WEDNESDAY, 22 JUNE

Something really strange happened at school today. Zoe and I were talking as we came out of the music room and Ben and Alex came walking up to us. Ben started talking to Zoe and she got all silly and giggly. I think she really likes him. But while Ben was talking with Zoe, Alex started talking to me. He asked me if I was going to the end of term dance. I didn't know what to say, so I just said "Probably."

He smiled back and said, "Me too, probably," and then they both walked off. When I told Tessa about it she laughed at me and said it looks like Alex might like me. I really don't know what to think but I kept smiling all night. Dad kept looking at me like he thought I was up to no good and all I could do was grin back, which I'm sure just convinced him even more that I was going to do something bad or that I was an idiot. Tessa gave me a funny wink. She can raise one eyebrow at a time like some actors do on the movies. If I try and do it I end up looking a right idiot and Dad would know for sure that something was up. Although there really isn't anything up, and I'm sure Alex was just being friendly while Zoe and Ben were talking, but it did make me feel good. I did think that Bella might be disappointed to hear Ben and Zoe were getting friendly, so I decided I would keep that to myself. I think a lot of girls like Ben.

FRIDAY, 24 JUNE

Both Zoe and I are having trouble remembering all the words to the songs we are doing. We are doing two songs as a duet, then we have three more with the whole choir. The kids in the orchestra have even more numbers to remember. Luckily, the dancers have CDs to dance to.

Zoe and I decided to skip practice today coz we're both getting annoyed with each other. I hid in the library and tried to do some of my homework but it was too noisy. I got a text from Laura to say she was going to be singing at assembly with her school choir. I felt really good for her, because I know she will be brilliant. If she was my duet partner, I know she'd push me harder to remember my words. I still want to do really well with Zoe, but for some reason, even though I'm trying hard with her, I know Laura would push me that bit more and I would remember my words. She would make me laugh, too, and that would help.

So I gave up on homework and listened to some music on my iPod. I was so into it I didn't hear the bell and the librarian got a bit cranky telling me to hurry up back to class. She also growled that I was not supposed to have an iPod at school so "don't let me catch you again or I will confiscate it."

All up, a pretty lame day.

SUNDAY, 26 JUNE

This afternoon I wrote all the lyrics I need to remember onto cardboard flash cards. I think if I practise just a few lines at a time, they'll eventually stick in my brain!

It's even harder remembering where I am supposed to stand and what actions I have to do. We can't just stand there in one spot looking stupid, so Zoe and I made up a little routine. It's a bit like a dance, but not really. It is just a few movements to help us flow better. I practised in front of the mirror in Mum's bedroom tonight. I still don't have a mirror in my room after mine smashed to bits in February's aftershock. Mum says it is a waste of money getting a new one when there are so many other things more important to replace. At least she lets me use hers.

FRIDAY, 1 JULY

OMG what a night! Aunty Beth and Uncle Dave came over and he was soooo angry. He waved a letter at Mum and Dad and told them to read it. Mum asked him to not wave it in her face and just tell them.

I was trying to pretend I was watching the TV and not really listening to them all, but it was something about their house being red-zoned residential and that it was "unlikely and uneconomical" to rebuild on their land. There was also something about the government making an offer for their property later. I tried to listen more but I think all I really got was Uncle Dave shouting that they've lost everything. Their home will be demolished and they'll have to find somewhere else to live.

I wanted to ask what would happen to all the birds in the Bexley Wetlands but I thought Uncle Dave might shout at me too, so I made some excuse and went to my room.

How sad. I love their house.

MONDAY, 4 JULY

Only 2 more weeks of school! Yay! I'm actually looking forward to the holidays, so I can just stay in bed and read. It is so cold in the mornings, and so dark. Winter is really here.

FRIDAY, 15 JULY
End of term dance

Couldn't wait for school to be over today so I could go home get ready for the dance – I'm wearing my new jeans and top. Dad picked up Bella too, so we could go to the dance together. Because the school hall was damaged in the February earthquake we couldn't have the dance there, but two of the classrooms have a big dividing wall between them that can be opened up. Usually it is kept locked so there are two separate classrooms, but now the caretaker has opened it up and piled up all the desks at one end. Mr Josephs rocks!

With coloured bed sheets over all the computers and the space decorated with helium balloons, huge big red bows and movie posters from the DVD shop, it looked really cool. Yay for the PTA!

Bella and I found a group of girls from our class and we hung out together at one end. The music was awesomely loud and we had to shout over it to hear each other. The girls danced at one end and the boys stood around talking at the other. Some of the boys looked like they wanted to dance but were too embarrassed. We laughed, because they did look a bit random standing there, wriggling in the corner. Zoe joined us, and I hate to admit it but her clothes were amazing. She had black tights and knee high boots with a tunic top over a long sleeved top that somehow made her look taller. But, man! Way too much make-up, which kind of ruined the look. It made her look like she was trying too hard.

Mum almost went ballistic when I put on some of Tessa's lipstick for the dance. "Maddy, you are only eleven years old and you will NOT leave this house wearing lipstick or any other make-up. You are too young and you look ridiculous. Take it off now. Do I make myself clear?" She almost yelled at me.

"I'm nearly twelve, and *everybody—*" I started, but she cut me off with a loud, "Maddy!'

I sighed and went and washed my face again, stamping my feet just to let her know I didn't think it was fair. Then Dad got in on the act and told me not to be rude to my mother or he wouldn't take me to the dance. UGH! Parents!

I did manage to convince Tessa to let me put on some mascara though. Just a little smidgen so Mum wouldn't notice. See? Again Tessa surprises me, helping me out even after Mum has laid down the law good and proper. I guess that makes Tessa an accessory to the crime – my crime. Well, only in Mum's laws. Actually, when I saw Zoe wearing all that make up I realised that maybe Mum was right, but I'd never tell her that. She'd never let me hear the end of it if I did.

Ben came over to talk to Zoe, and then Alex came over to talk to Ben ... then he started talking to Bella and me. And that is how we spent the rest of the night, just a little group of us, talking and laughing. Well, *shouting* and laughing. By the end of the night I had hardly any voice left and my ears were still ringing when I went to bed. But it was a brilliant way to end the school term.

MONDAY, 25 JULY

It's snowing! Seriously snowing! Not just a sprinkling of sleet but fresh white snow falling everywhere. There is just so much of it! I don't ever remember this much before. It is so beautiful I can't take my eyes off it. Jackson and I started building a snowman and eventually Tessa and Mum joined in too. Tessa tripped over and fell flat on her face in the snow. Talk about funny! I laughed and she started chasing me – I thought she was going to throttle me but then she burst out laughing too.

It was awesome to see so much snow. It's still snowing as I am trying to go to bed, but I can't sleep. It is so exciting to see this much snow. I can't see the lawn or road at all any more. Everywhere and everything is white. The snow has even clung to the clothesline, hanging there so thick the pegs are completely hidden. Even in the dark the snow stands out all shiny and new. And it is so quiet and still. It is truly beautiful.

TUESDAY, 26 JULY

The snow is now so deep it's almost past the tops of my gumboots. Jackson looks like a yeti buried in the snow up to his neck. We spent the day building an enormous snowman on the front lawn. The wee kids from down the road where Tessa sometimes babysits came down with their mum and we all kept making the snowman bigger and bigger. Then we had snow fights and made snow angels – all different sizes. Awesome fun.

Mum got a call from Aunty Beth to say the weight of the snow on the roof of her house was so bad that the roof was leaking through the cracks, but luckily it was in the spare room so they'd put tarpaulins on the carpet to protect the floor. Mum told her there was no point worrying about it because the house was going to come down anyway when they start demolishing the suburb. Aunty Beth must've got mad because Mum's voice was getting louder.

Jackson gets upset now when people start arguing. I could tell he was about to cry so I threw at snowball at him and called out "Ha-ha, you can't catch me."

Good distraction. He started chucking snowballs at me and chasing me. Mostly he missed but I copped one right on my nose. Yeow! And oh so cold!

By the end of the day we were really tired and wet. Thank goodness we had power because all the clothes just went straight into the washing machine and then the dryer. Some places have a power cut. How cold would that be with all that snow? I'm glad it isn't us. I took a heap of photos. So did lots of other people and put them all up on YouTube. Things end up on the internet so fast these days, but the snow ones were magic. It kind of makes it feel as though everyone in the world knows we've got snow. This is our heaviest snowfall in something like 20 years. Amazing! But today everything looked beautiful, just like in a fairy tale.

It felt so good to get in to bed tonight and stick my toes on my hot water bottle and then snuggle down under the blankets and duvet.

WEDNESDAY, 27 JULY

Guess what? I slept all through the night for the first time in ages. And Dusty was curled up beside me the whole night.

The snow is still everywhere and roads are blocked and the council's telling people to drive only if they have to. Our snowman hasn't melted at all. In fact, the snow has gone from that soft powdery stuff to being like ice. On the road where the cars have been driving down the middle it's all slush but the sides still have snow piled up.

Some of our neighbours have been out digging the snow off their driveways so Mum told us we had to do ours. Jackson thought it was fun for all of five minutes and Tessa just grumbled something about it not being fair, especially since Dad is out helping clear the roads in the city instead of being here to help his own family. I told her to grow up and she stormed inside. Mum sent her straight back out and we dug the drive in silence. We dug and scraped the snow from the area where the tyres would go and left the rest so it looked quite cool really.

SATURDAY, 30 JULY

The snow is almost gone except in sheltered places where the sun hasn't found it yet. Strange to think we had so much snow that even five days later it's still hanging around in places. I was outside in the garden looking for Dusty when I noticed, under the last of the snow, some small bits of green poking through the soil. It was just the tiniest early peeking of Mum's daffodils. Way too early and only the tiniest hint of green, but I knew straight away what they were. And then I began to cry. Really cry and I couldn't stop. That's where Mum found me with tears running down my cheeks.

"Maddy, what's wrong, love?"

"Look Mum." I pointed to the buds.

She pulled me close and hugged me and she had tears too now and I knew she felt just the way I did. Those tiny little buds are hope. Green coloured hope. This is a sign that things are going to get better. I just know it. I know that we will be okay. Not just my family, but all of us in Christchurch. Maybe not today, maybe not tomorrow, but whatever happens I just know we are going to be all right.

It has been the most awful, terrifying and tragic year where 185 people were killed, and hundreds more injured. It is a year where my city has fallen. My city has crashed to its knees and everywhere we look, everywhere we go, we see reminders of the damage: fallen houses and broken roads in our broken city.

But those buds today are just the most beautiful things I have seen in a long time. Even under the frozen earth, they are trying to poke their little heads through, wanting to reach for the sun. I went inside and gave Tessa and Jackson a big hug. They both looked at me like I was crazy but I don't care ... and when Dad gets home tonight, I'm going to give him a big hug too. And I'm going to ring Gran after dinner. Even if I can't give her a hug, I can talk to her.

Anyway, it's only two weeks until my birthday and Laura will be coming up for the weekend. I can't wait. And maybe she will be coming back to stay and everything will be okay. She might not, but I have my fingers crossed because in this crazy, horrible year anything is possible.

And another thing – I don't care who I sing with in the school production next term. I know I can do it. I know I will remember the words and I know it will be all right.

Photo courtesy GNS Science Te Pū Ao

At 6.3 magnitude, the destructive February 2011 earthquake was less than September 2010's 7.1 quake, but struck closer to Christchurch.

HISTORICAL NOTE

At 4.35 a.m. on 4 September 2010, a magnitude 7.1 earthquake split the night with a deafening roar and rumble that shook everyone out of bed, damaged homes and left a path of destruction. It was recorded at a depth of 10 kilometres near Darfield, 30 kilometres from the centre of Christchurch.

While devastating and destructive, it did not cause any deaths. Cantabrians could not believe the fortunate timing of the earthquake and the fact that most places were closed and few people were out and about. They could not believe that no one had died in such a massive earthquake. They were lucky and they knew it.

It did begin, however, a sequence of aftershocks that eventually changed the face of the Christchurch and Canterbury Region forever. Little did people know what would follow, on 22 February at 12.51 p.m. A much shallower and more devastating earthquake destroyed the city centre, demolishing many heritage buildings and leaving thousands of homes damaged beyond repair. It took the lives of 185 people. February's aftershock was centred 10 kilometres southeast of the Central Business District, near Lyttelton, and was only 5 kilometres deep.

The damage was beyond comprehension. Amputations were performed on the injured while still trapped under rubble. The injured were carried in the backs of cars or on foot to makeshift emergency centres.

A week after the February quake, 35 percent of the city was still without water and 36,000 households still had no power.

It was different from other aftershocks and packed a punch far more powerful and tragic. It had both vertical and horizontal movement, which means that not only was the ground shaking things from side to side, but a 'trampoline' effect meant things were also lifted up and dropped back down. Not everything could survive the impact and many of the city's stone and brick historic buildings were damaged beyond repair. Many have now been demolished, leaving a barren landscape where once the heart of the city stood proud. The damage to the Christchurch Cathedral in particular, has stood symbolically as a reminder for the grief and loss that thousands of Cantabrians have endured.

Many people have left the city; their children are enrolled in schools outside Christchurch. Some have returned but some never will. The memory is too dark and despairing.

It will remain one of New Zealand's biggest and most tragic natural disasters. Even in 2014 the daily life in such a severely damaged city continues to challenge those that remain. There are delays everywhere, traffic congestions, road works and road cones throughout the suburbs. There are still houses waiting for repairs and the demolitions continue. The skyline of the CBD has changed markedly, and in place of high-rise buildings we see cranes tearing down buildings.

Suburbs have also come under attack and many will be torn apart, forcing people from homes and communities they have lived in for years. For example, the Pacific Park suburb, which backed onto the beautiful wetlands in Bexley. The whole suburb is being demolished and will not be rebuilt as the land is too unstable and too prone to liquefaction. The whole community has been displaced and it is this loss that causes much grief.

There have been over 12,000 aftershocks since that early September morning in 2010. The landmark clock on the Science Alive building, once the home of Christchurch's Railway Station, stopped at exactly 4.35 a.m., reminding everyone of what had happened. This building has since been demolished.

During the Christmas season of 2011 people placed festive tinsel over the road cones that lined so many streets. It was a thoughtful gesture that brought smiles to many faces. Christmas trees were placed on deserted sites and decorated. Everyone tried to remain positive and festive. It had been a year unlike any other in New Zealand. Christchurch had suffered four major earthquakes, thousands of aftershocks and two of the worst snowstorms in decades.

The people of Christchurch and the surrounding area lost much of their heritage and much of what made their city unique, but most did not lose hope. Nothing will ever replace the lost lives nor wipe away the grief which remains heavy in the air, but people are hopeful and determined that the rebuild will see a stronger and better city grow out of the tragedy and destruction.

Kia kaha, Christchurch.

Martin Hunter, iStock

The historic Deans Homestead in Home Bush, Canterbury, (where some of the movie *The Lion, the Witch and the Wardrobe* was filmed in 2005) was irreparably damaged in the September 2010 quake.

Many of Christchurch's old stone buildings (such as the Provincial Chambers pictured), which gave the city its character, tumbled down in the earthquakes.

Shelves in The Children' Bookshop emptied themselves during the September earthquake.

Photos courtesy Jenny Cooper

The quake caused liquefaction to bubble up through the earth's crust, creating sink holes. As it dried out, it became a thick, heavy grey sludge.

Houses in many suburbs were surrounded by thick liquefaction, and family and friends – sometimes even diggers – were brought in to help clear it off roads and properties.

Huge boulders were dislodged and tumbled down hills – one even crashed straight through the middle of this house and out the other side!

Photo courtesy Jenny Cooper

Much of Christchurch's CBD was devastated in the February 2011 quake. This was one of the city's main shopping areas, Colombo Street.

Giant cracks opened up in roads all over the region, making travel hazardous. This man is 1.95 metres tall!

The Medway footbridge was left twisted and mangled after the quake.

Army troops pump water from the sea to desalinate for household use.

Even in extreme circumstances, children will find ways to have fun, building 'sand' castles out of liquefaction, and using broken roads as BMX ramps!

GLOSSARY

Aftershock: small earthquake or tremor that follows a large earthquake

Epicentre: the area on the earth's surface above where the earthquake started; most damage occurs near the epicentre

EQC: Earthquake Commission (government department)

Fault line: a fracture along which the earth's crust has moved

Liquefaction: during an earthquake some loose soil below the surface is shaken so much that it becomes like liquid and bubbles up through the surface where it settles and becomes a heavy, thick grey sludge

Magnitude: the amount of energy released in an earthquake. It is decided by the severity of the shaking, which is recorded on a seismograph.

MMI (Modified Mercalli intensity): a measurement of the impact of an earthquake on people, marked on a scale of 1–12

Seismic waves: waves of energy that spread out from the epicentre of an earthquake

UCSVA: University of Canterbury Student Volunteer Army – the thousands of students who banded together and worked very hard over a number of months cleaning up liquefaction in Christchurch

Desna Wallace

WEB SITES

http://www.gns.cri.nz/Home/Learning/Science-Topics/
Earthquakes/Earthquakes-and-Faults

Provides easy to understand information on earthquakes and faults.

http://info.geonet.org.nz/display/quake/Shaking+Intensity

Explains the Modified Mercalli intensity scale.

http://canterburyquakelive.co.nz/

A site that displays the earthquakes recorded by GeoNet, a
geological hazard monitoring system in New Zealand that
detects, analyses and responds to earthquakes, volcanic
activity, large landslides, tsunami and the slow deformation that
precedes large earthquakes.